It all happened ~~~~~~~~~~~~~~~~~ **was gone, his hands** ~~~~~~~~~~~~~~~ **ning up against her b**~~~~~~~~~~~~~~~**a towel to her near nakedness, staring into the eyes of a man who looked shell-shocked.**

What in the hell was he doing here? He had twelve security personnel scoping the property, a car waiting and a jet on the tarmac at Heathrow, and he, Alexei Ranaevsky, was seducing the nanny in an upstairs bedroom.

And doing a spectacularly lousy job of it.

"Maisy." He spoke her name abruptly.

"You haven't changed your mind?" she challenged with what nerve she had left, strengthening her voice with the knowledge that Kostya came first. "About me coming. With Kostya."

For a moment he actually looked confused, as if she had said something completely out of left field, when it was the only thing that mattered, wasn't it? Then he sighed and ran a hand over his unshaven face.

"No, I haven't changed my mind," he muttered, "God help me, I haven't changed my mind."

All about the author…
Lucy Ellis

LUCY ELLIS has four loves in life: books, expensive lingerie, vintage films and big gorgeous men who have to duck going through doorways. Weaving aspects of them into her fiction is the best part of being a romance writer. Lucy lives in a small cottage in the foothills outside Melbourne.

Innocent in the Ivory Tower is Lucy Ellis's first novel for the Harlequin Presents® line, and we hope you love it as much as we do!

Lucy Ellis

INNOCENT IN THE IVORY TOWER

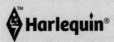

TORONTO NEW YORK LONDON
AMSTERDAM PARIS SYDNEY HAMBURG
STOCKHOLM ATHENS TOKYO MILAN MADRID
PRAGUE WARSAW BUDAPEST AUCKLAND

Recycling programs
for this product may
not exist in your area.

ISBN-13: 978-0-373-13063-4

INNOCENT IN THE IVORY TOWER

First North American Publication 2012

www.Harlequin.com

Printed in U.S.A.

INNOCENT IN THE IVORY TOWER

For Martha

CHAPTER ONE

ALEXEI RANAEVSKY strode across the light-filled environs of his floating boardroom and picked up the newspaper one of his staff had been careless enough to leave behind.

He had made it clear he wanted to see no reportage of the Kulikov tragedy, but now the initial shock was wearing off he found himself drawn to what could only be described as the circus that was attaching itself to events. How to dismantle that circus was his current concern.

How to grieve for his closest friend would come after.

Events had moved to the third page. A picture of Leo and Anais at a race meeting in Dubai, Leo's head thrown back, laughing, his arm welded around Anais's slender waist. A golden couple. Alongside was exactly what Alexei didn't want to see: a photograph of the mangled car wreck. The 1967 Aston Martin—Leo's 'baby'—nothing more than steel and destroyed electronics. Leo and Anais's very human bodies hadn't stood a chance.

The commentary below—because you couldn't call it news—was adjective-heavy, full of references to Anais's beauty and Leo's work for the UN. Alexei scanned it for a few seconds, then sucked in a sharp breath.

Konstantine Kulikov.

Kostya.

There was something about seeing that name in print that made what had felt for days now like a nightmare fiercely, immediately real. At least there was no picture of the boy. Leo had been intensely guarded about their private life: he and Anais had been fair game for the media, but their family life had been off-limits to anyone outside their circle. It was a sentiment Alexei admired him for. It was a rule he laid down in his own life. There was the public man, and the private *familya*, and the fact that Leo had been that family for him made his grief all the more stupefying.

'Alexei?'

His head snapped up, jaw hard, eyes emotionless.

For a second her name evaded him. 'Tara,' he said.

If she noticed the lapse it did not register on her stunning face. It was a face that was currently making her several million dollars a year in beauty endorsements, in lieu of an acting career that had gone nowhere.

'Everyone's waiting, darling,' she said smoothly, crossing the space between them and pulling the newspaper out of his hands.

It was the wrong thing to do.

He had never struck a woman in his life, and he had no intention of starting now, but every fibre of his body wanted to lash out. Instead he froze. Tara lifted her chin defiantly. She was nothing if not bold—and wasn't that what had drawn him to her?

'You don't need to look at that trash,' she said harshly. 'You need to pull it together and get out there and put a civilised face on this whole debacle.'

Everything she said was everything he knew, but something—some important mechanism between his brain and his emotions—had snapped. Many would say he didn't have any emotions, not real ones. He certainly hadn't cried for Leo and Anais. He hadn't even cried for his own dead parents. But there was something surging through him that his brain wasn't going to be able to control. Something that had its wellspring in that child's name in black-and-white in newspaper ink.

Kostya.

Orphaned.

Alone.

Tara's 'debacle'.

'Let them wait,' he said coldly, his English coloured by his Russian accent. 'And what in the hell are you wearing? This isn't a cocktail party—it's a family gathering.'

Tara snorted laughter. It was one of the traits he had once found appealing about her, her lack of self-consciousness—as if her overwhelming physical beauty made it possible for her to say anything, do anything, be anything.

'Family? Give me a break—those people aren't your family.' She reached out and pressed her red-taloned hand to his waist, taut beneath the expensively tailored cream shirt. 'You have as much family feeling as a cat, Alexei,' she stated, face upturned, lips wet and red, her hand making its way down the front of his dark trousers. 'A big, mean, feral cat. *Very* big.' Her hand settled on what she found there. 'Not up to play today, darling?'

His body had begun to respond as long familiarity with the process had taught it, but sex was not on today's agenda. It hadn't been on the agenda since Monday, when his right-hand man, Carlo, had brought him the news in the early hours. He remembered the snapping on of the lamp, Carlo's murmured voice as he laid out the spare, basic facts such as they had been. Then he had been alone in that big flat bed, swimming in emptiness. Tara had been beside him, dead to the world under a blanket of whatever drugs she took to sleep. A body.

He had been alone.

I never want to have sex with this woman ever again.

He grasped her forearm and gently but with leashed force revolved her one hundred and eighty degrees to face the door.

'Off you go,' he murmured in her ear, as if imparting an endearment—only his voice was completely dead of feeling. 'Join them on deck. Don't drink too much, and here.' He picked up the newspaper she had dropped on the boardroom table. 'Dispose of this.'

Tara had been in the wide world long enough to know she

was experiencing the infamous Ranaevsky Chill Factor. She just hadn't expected to feel it herself, or perhaps not quite so soon.

'Danni was right. You *are* a cold bastard.'

Alexei didn't have a clue who Danni was—didn't particularly care. He just wanted Tara out of the room. Out of his life.

He wanted the people outside off his boat.

He wanted to turn the clock back to Sunday.

Mostly he wanted his control back. Control over the situation.

'How in the hell are you going to raise a child?' Tara snarled as she strutted out through the door.

Control. His dark eyes fixed on the Florida coastline, visible through the wraparound windows. He would begin by doing what he needed to do. Speaking to the people outside. Speaking to Carlo. Most of all speaking to Kostya, a two-year-old infant. But first he needed to fly across the Atlantic to do it.

"'The owl and the pussycat went to sea in a beautiful pea-green boat,'" sang Maisy in a soft contralto, her body arced over the small boy curled on his side in the crib. He had been sucking on the plump flesh of his fist, but as sleep claimed him his pink mouth closed and presently his barrel-shaped chest rose and fell beneath the delicate ribbed cotton singlet he wore.

She had been singing to him for a while now, after a full half-hour of reading, and her throat felt dry, her voice slightly hoarse. But it was worth it to see him like this, so peaceful.

Standing up, she scanned the room, checking everything was in its place. The nursery was as it had always been— a place of womblike security—yet everything outside it had changed. For this little boy, for ever.

Tiptoeing out, she closed the door. The baby monitor was on and she knew from experience he would sleep now until after midnight. It was her chance to get some food and then some sleep herself. She'd been awake so much of the past thirty-six hours she couldn't even gauge how much sleep she'd had.

Two floors down, the kitchen was dimly lit. Valerie, the Kulikovs' housekeeper, had left the spotlights over the benches on for her, and they cast an almost ghostly glow. Valerie had also left a dish of macaroni and cheese in the fridge to be re-heated, and Maisy silently thanked her as she slid the bowl into the microwave.

The older woman had been a godsend this week. When the news had come through of the crash Maisy had been in her room, packing for a vacation that was due to start on Tuesday. She remembered putting down the telephone and sitting by it for a full ten minutes before she even thought of what to do next. Then she had rung Valerie and life had resumed movement.

She and Valerie had both expected Leo and Anais's families to sweep in, but the house in the private London square had remained silent. Inside, Valerie continued to do her hours and return to her family at night, and Maisy cared for her charge and waited for the plea that had not yet come. *I want Mama.*

The press had been there for a couple of days, pushing up at the windows, clambering over the iron railings to drop to the basement. Valerie had kept the blinds drawn, and Maisy had only taken Kostya out once, to the private garden across the road. Maisy had worked for the Kulikovs since Kostya's birth, and lived in this house all that time. Leo and Anais had travelled frequently. Maisy was accustomed to being alone with Kostya for weeks at a time. Yet there was something—empty—tonight. The house felt too quiet, and Maisy found herself jumping as the microwave pinged, pressing open the door with a hand that trembled.

Get a grip, she told herself sternly, using an oven mitt to carry the bowl over to the big French provincial table. She didn't bother to turn on the main light. There was something comforting about the darkness.

Steam rose off the macaroni. She ought to be hungry, and

she needed to keep her strength up. Her fork made a cruise around the edges. In her mind's eye she could still see Anais in this very room a week ago, laughing in that full-throated way at a drawing Kostya had done in crayon on the floor tiles of a giraffe with a head like his mummy's. Anais had been almost six feet tall, and mostly legs, which had been the focus of her modelling career. It was clearly how her little son had seen her from his diminutive position.

Maisy remembered the first time she had met Anais. She had been a small, dumpy swot, detailed by her headmistress to introduce the skinny, impossibly tall Anais Parker-Stone to the rituals of St Bernice's. Anais hadn't known then that Maisy Edmonds was a charity girl, her place in the very exclusive girls' school arranged for her on a government programme. When she had found out, Anais hadn't changed her allegiances. If Maisy had been ostracised for her background, Anais had been victimised for her height.

For two years the girls had been close friends, until Anais dropped out at sixteen and four months later had started modelling in New York. Two years later she was famous.

As Maisy had matured she'd lost her puppy fat, gained a waist and some length in her legs, and her curves had become an asset. She had gone on to university but dropped out before the first term had even begun. Her only contact with Anais had been via the glossy magazines Anais stalked through. When Maisy had run into her at Harrods it had been Anais who'd recognised her—probably because she had hardly changed, Maisy thought ruefully.

Anais, all sleek blonde bob and three-inch heels, had shrieked with joy, thrown her skinny arms around Maisy's small shoulders and jumped up and down like a teenage girl. A teenage girl with a baby bump. Three months later Maisy had been ensconced in Lantern Square, with a newborn baby in her arms and a completely overwhelmed Anais weeping and threatening to kill herself and trying to escape the house every chance she could. Nobody had ever told her motherhood wasn't a job she could walk away from, that it was for life.

A far too short life, as it had turned out, Maisy thought heavily and stopped pretending to eat. She pushed the plate away. She had cried for her friend, and she had cried for tiny Kostya. She imagined at some point those tears would dry up. Right now it seemed they had.

She had more pressing considerations.

Any day now a lawyer for the Kulikovs, although more likely for the Parker-Stones, would land on the doorstep. People who would take away Kostya. Maisy knew nothing about the Kulikovs other than that Leo had been an only child and his parents were deceased. But she remembered Arabella Parker-Stone, who had seen her grandson once, a few days after his birth. It had been a brief visit, involving calla lilies and harsh words between Anais and her mother.

'I hate her, I hate her, I hate her,' Anais had wailed afterwards into a sofa cushion, whilst Maisy rocked Kostya in her arms.

Arabella had upset everyone. But her mind was failing and she was now in a nursing home. Kostya would *not* be going to live with his grandmother.

Nor will he be living with me.

Maisy didn't know how she was going to hand Kostya over to strangers. Wild thoughts of simply absconding with him had crossed her mind yesterday and today. It all seemed possible, with the world ignoring them, but once it paid attention how on earth would she manage it? She was jobless and her only skill was as a carer for the infirm, the elderly, or the very young. Her *vocation* was loving that little boy upstairs. He had become her family—but, more painfully, she was his. Somehow she had to find a way to stay with him. Surely whoever stepped forward would need a nanny? Would not be so cruel as to separate them…?

Maisy took a deep breath and pushed the hair out of her face. She reeled her bowl back in and, head resting on one hand, picked at a first mouthful of pasta, munching by rote. She needed sustenance; this would give it to her. Tomorrow she would have to go through Leo's office and phone people. Such had been his mania for privacy, very few outsiders had been in this house. Anais had never complained—she had merely gone out. Another excuse to leave her son. Maisy had never understood Anais's inability to bond with Kostya, but she had excused it.

And now it just didn't matter any more.

It was a movement, not a sound, that pulled her out of her miserable thoughts with an abrupt jab of adrenaline. Something shifted at the corner of her vision and her head jerked up, her shoulders pulling tight as twine.

Someone was in the house.

She froze, listening intently.

In that moment two men stepped out of the pooling darkness beyond the island bench, and as she processed their presence the room filled up with men. Three more came rushing down the stairs, and another two bursting through the garden entrance. That they all seemed to be wearing suits brought Maisy no comfort as the spoon dropped from her hand and she stumbled backwards out of her chair.

The shortest of the thugs came towards her and said, 'Hands behind your head. Get on the floor.'

But a bigger man—taller, leaner, younger—brushed him aside and said something brusquely in a foreign language.

Maisy stared open mouthed at him, shock rooting her to the spot and he swore.

'English, Alexei Fedorovich,' said another of the men, almost as terrifying with his height and bulk.

Oh, God, it was the Russian mafia.

The hysterical thought coincided with the younger man making a sudden movement towards her, and Maisy's body reacted to protect itself.

She grabbed the chair and threw it with all her might at him. Then she screamed.

CHAPTER TWO

'ALEXEI,' said a voice at his elbow. 'Perhaps we should wait.'

Alexei barely spared a glance for his factotum Carlo Santini. He didn't do waiting.

The first thing he'd noticed about the house was that the security code hadn't been changed. Clearly no one was in charge. The second had been the almost abnormal silence of the house. It was close on midnight, but there was a closed-up feeling to the rooms. His hackles raised, he'd headed towards a pale light gleaming from the stairwell leading downstairs into the basement. His godson had been alone for four days, and he wanted to see for himself the situation he was walking into. Although his security would move up through the house from basement to attic, he knew it would be easier to cut to the chase himself.

He had spotted her immediately—a shapeless figure hunched over a bowl, sitting in the dark. Good—staff. As he'd walked across the room she had seemed to sense him, because her head had come up and for a moment he'd been thrown by the vulnerability that softened her dimly lit features as she'd sought to make sense of his presence. He'd had a further impression of fragility and femininity, despite the clothes that enveloped her.

In that moment the French doors had exploded open in front of him and more personnel had come thundering down the stairs behind him. The woman had reacted like a loaded gun. They were protecting *him*, but she wasn't to know that.

The trigger for this overreaction had heaved her chair and

dived under the table, rolling herself into a ball. Now, Alexei cursed and shoved the table over a few feet, hauled her up into his arms, registering her real terror as she began to kick and struggle against him. Better him than one of his security detail, who would be less inclined to go gently with her.

His muttered imprecations and rough assurances of, 'I am not going to hurt you,' did little to stem her reaction—until he realised in his exhausted state he was using Russian. 'Calm yourself,' he said distinctly in English. 'No one wishes you any harm.'

Maisy jerked her head sideways and her eyes welded to his. They were deep blue, heavily lashed and stunning. His cheekbones were like scimitars, and she recognised that faint upsweep of his bone structure as Slavic.

He clearly hadn't shaved in many days, but otherwise he smelled good. Maisy's body recognised this as her mind struggled to keep up. His cologne filled her nostrils, along with the subtler but more enticing smell of him—warm, male flesh. She could feel the fight slipping out of her body as her senses told her this man truly meant her no harm, even as those same senses began to be overloaded with other messages.

Alexei sensed the change in her. She was no longer a victim fighting back but a woman in his arms, waiting for him to make a move. He reluctantly set her down, but kept one hand fastened over her shoulder, holding her in place. He didn't want his security detail marching her off, possibly manhandling her. He didn't question why other men touching her filled him with the primitive urge to protect her. He was tired, and he hadn't had sex, and he was in the mood to tear down the house if he didn't get that child.

'Talk to her,' he said, the weight of his hand lifting from her shoulder.

Feeling suddenly adrift, Maisy looked up to face another man—shorter, slighter, perhaps a decade older and sharply dressed—who stepped forward and inclined his head rather formally.

'Good evening, *signorina*. I apologise for the intrusion. I am Carlo. I work for Alexei Ranaevsky.'

Maisy's head swivelled back to the younger man. He wasn't even listening. He had retrieved a phone from his jacket and was reading whatever messages it contained.

This was talking to her?

'Try Spanish,' was all he said, in a deep, gravelly voice she hadn't registered before when he had spoken in Russian.

Maisy sat through Spanish, Italian and interestingly Polish renditions of the same introduction. As the Polish rolled musically on she tried to marshal her racing thoughts. Her gaze kept creeping back to the man who had restrained her. He seemed to be the focus in the room, and he reeked confidence and control. Except when she had been in his arms for a moment there she had sensed something else. Something very much uncontrolled.

Maisy suppressed an involuntary shiver and his head came up, as if sensing her movement. His darkened eyes moved over her, settling on the pulse that was beating wildly at the base of her throat. It held his assessing gaze for a moment. Then he said abruptly, 'She's English.'

He despatched the mobile and gave her a measured look.

'I need to know where the boy is.'

Maisy's skittering pulse went still. Every hackle in her body rose.

Alexei saw the moment she shut down, and cursed himself inwardly. He didn't have time for this. When she didn't answer he lost patience. 'I'm taking Leonid Kulikov's son out of here. I need you to take me to him.'

'No,' she said.

No? *No?* Alexei made a soft sound of disbelief.

'I'm not letting you anywhere near the Kulikovs' child. Who in the *hell* do you think you are?'

The kitten could scratch. Despite himself, Alexei felt his libido give a little kick.

'I'm Alexei Ranaevsky, his legal guardian.'

Her gaze made an involuntary skate over the breadth of his chest and shoulders, then fastened on his face. He had dark hair, curling and close-cropped, and he was about as close to a fantasy as Maisy had ever had.

Yet her stomach twisted, even as she knew she ought to feel relief.

Someone had finally come for Kostya. But because no one was walking Kostya out of this house without *her*, this man had come for her too. Only he didn't know it. Something fluttered low in Maisy's chest and she recognised it was fear—quite different from the terror she had felt when these men had burst in on her. This was fear of the known.

Alexei had apparently said everything he was going to say to her, and turned around and headed for the stairs.

Maisy's anxious 'Wait!' didn't break his stride.

She chased him up two flights of stairs, all the while babbling about not waking Kostya, but he ignored her completely.

Why isn't he listening to me?

He'd reached the nursery landing when she launched herself at him physically. 'Please. Stop.'

Alexei paused midstride as female arms came around his waist. Bumping up against him, she grappled to take hold of his jacket. She was panting, and Alexei looked down to see some of her curls had come loose. With the colour high in her cheeks she was considerably more intriguing than she had been at first glance. She was also clearly very distressed.

But that was not his concern, Alexei dismissed irritably. She knew who he was. She was either trying to garner his attention or behaving irrationally. Either was of no interest to him. He moved and she didn't, and a very decisive ripping sound rent the air between them.

There was an awful moment as Maisy realised what she had done. His eyes locked on hers, whatever he'd been about to say giving way to a look of complete disbelief. Satisfaction at finally gaining his attention turned up the corners of Maisy's lips, and his stare dropped to the lush unpainted pink of her mouth and buzzed there.

Disconcerted, she lost her concentration for a moment, and something of this must have communicated itself because an answering smile hovered over his mouth. Struck, Maisy dropped her gaze and, making the most of her advantage in that moment, moved fast, scooting ahead of him and blocking his way as best she could.

'I am not letting you see Kostya until you tell me what's going on.'

His gaze ran the length of her, and his tone was an arctic degree cooler than his eyes. 'You're in full possession of the facts. I'm his legal guardian. Remove yourself.'

As if that was all he had to say.

'Or what? You'll get one of your bully boys to do it for you?' Maisy challenged. Some part of her brain told her this was *not* persuading him she was the right person to look after Kostya, but he was making her so angry with his high-handed attitude. It wasn't his house. Kostya wasn't his child. And she certainly wasn't his doormat.

'Do you cook here? Clean?' he rapped out. 'Because, quite frankly, I don't explain my actions to staff.'

'I'm the nanny,' she flung at him—which was close enough to the truth.

He swore under his breath, those blue eyes narrowing suspiciously on her. 'Why in the hell didn't you say so earlier?'

'I wasn't sure what was going on.'

It sounded lame even as she said it. She couldn't very well say, *You put your arms around me and I felt your body and I got thoroughly distracted, and then I saw your face and you reduced me to a puddle of wanting woman.* Because she darn well knew it probably happened to him every other day.

Maisy moistened her lips, drawing herself up to her full height of five feet four inches. 'I want you to hold on and explain to me exactly what you intend doing.' Her voice sounded high and breathless, and unlikely to get her a response from this hard man.

He didn't look ready to explain. He looked as if he wanted to shake her. He looked as if he couldn't believe he was having this—*any*—conversation with her. A child's wail broke the stalemate.

'Konstantine.'

'Kostya.'

They both spoke at once. Maisy dared him with her eyes to push her aside and he hesitated, clearly not wanting to let her pass but less sure about how gung-ho he should be with a two-year-old infant.

Maisy seized the opportunity and went first, but she could sense him close behind her all the way. She hesitated at the nursery door, then swung around and almost bumped her nose on his hard chest. His big body tensed and she cringed. She had to stop touching him. He'd think there was something wrong with her. Yet already a reactive shiver of response was running the length of her body and she instinctively took a step back.

'Listen,' she said, groping for composure. 'You will stay out here. He'll only be frightened if he sees a strange man.'

He inclined his head. 'I will wait.'

Maisy ducked into the room, dimly lit by a night lamp near the cot. Kostya was standing in the middle of the mattress, face red and wet as his cries died away on a last wail when he saw what he wanted. Maisy. His chubby arms extended trustfully towards her and Maisy closed the distance between them in an instant.

'Maisy!' he enunciated clearly.

She struggled with lifting him. He was big for his age, and in another year she would have difficulty carrying him in her arms. She felt for the armchair behind her and slid into it, cradling the warm little body in her arms.

Alexei stood watching them. He hadn't expected to be moved in any way by the sight of the child in a woman's arms. She seemed at ease in a way he knew he could never be with such a small child. He supposed it came naturally for some women, being maternal; it had certainly not been a natural function of any of the women he knew. In fact he struggled, now he thought about it, to come up with any woman he'd been with who was comfortable around children.

Which was something he had in common with them. He definitely had no interest in his friends' kids. He'd been god-father to Konstantine for two years and seen the child once: on the day he'd stood up for him in the Russian Orthodox Church here in London.

'I didn't know he would be so…small,' Alexei said quietly, not wanting to startle the child.

Maisy smoothed her hand over the back of Kostya's res-tive head as the little boy peered around to see where the male voice had come from. It was a voice that sounded somewhat like his father's, Maisy registered. A shade deeper, but with the irregular emphasis on vowels that revealed English was a second language for him.

'Papa,' he said uncertainly, in his clear, high child's voice.

'No, it's not Papa,' Maisy said softly, her tongue sticking to the roof of her mouth.

He came slowly towards them and dropped down beside the chair, so that his height and bulk were no longer frightening, and said in a grave voice, 'Hello, Kostya. I am your godfather, Alexei Ranaevsky.'

Some of the tension Maisy was holding in her body shifted and melted with those words. Kostya's godfather. Why hadn't she remembered? The day of Kostya's christening she had been in bed with a fever, but the au pair girl had brought back a gushing description of the *über*cool Alexei Ranaevsky, and here he was—in the flesh.

He lifted those megawatt blue eyes to her and said quietly, 'You will get him back to sleep and I will wait for you outside.'

The velvet of his voice brushed over her. Maisy recognised his words as a directive and wondered if Alexei Ranaevsky ever asked permission for anything.

When she emerged the house felt empty again. The security detail had evaporated, although Maisy doubted they were far away. She stood at the top of the stairwell, listening for movement.

'Here,' came a deep voice from across the landing.

Maisy followed it into her own room. She hesitated on the threshold. Alexei was standing by the window, somehow managing to fill the entire room with his presence. Amidst the delicately feminine decor of duck-egg-blue and white he looked absurdly out of place.

'Sit down,' was all he said.

'I'd rather stand...'

'Sit down.'

Maisy rolled her eyes and sat on her narrow bed. He began to walk around, lifting framed photos, knick-knacks, even examining an atomiser of the perfume Maisy usually wore. All the while his attention seemed to be on her, and it was disconcerting. His raw energy was starting to roll through her and Maisy shifted on the bed, wishing she hadn't sat down.

Alexei rubbed his chin ruefully and wondered why it was that after four days of abstinence, and a total lack of interest in sex for the first time in his adult life, it had all come roaring back the minute his body made contact with hers.

Looking at her now, it seemed she didn't appear to have a waist under all that wool, but he remembered the curve of it under his hands. In the same way he knew her breasts would be soft and round and her hips and bottom lush in his hands. Her hair was much longer than it looked—she had it all caught up—and it would be long and curling. He could bury his hands in it when she was on her knees to him...

He almost growled with frustration. What was it about death and sex? Maybe that was why his body had gone there and his head had followed. Leo was dead. Leo's child was now his lifetime responsibility, and he took his responsibilities seriously. Sitting in front of him was something both life-affirming and yet not serious at all. Sex with a real woman—not a sprayed, painted, waxed, plastic actress/model perfume commercial. Hell, she wasn't even wearing make-up. She didn't really need it, she had great skin, and that hair…

Suddenly she stood up. 'Mr Ranaevsky—'

'Alexei,' he offered.

'Alexei.'

She took a deep breath, and he registered she was about to make some sort of speech. That was never good.

'I didn't catch your name.'

'Maisy. Maisy Edmonds.'

Maisy.

'Sit down, Maisy.'

'No, I need to say this standing up.'

'Sit down.'

She sat. It was a good sign. Pliable.

She stood up. 'No, this is important. I want to come with Kostya. I don't know what your circumstances are, or what you have organised, but I want to stay with him until he's settled. And he doesn't know yet. When he's told, I need to be there.'

Alexei frowned heavily. 'He doesn't know his parents are dead?'

Maisy shook her head, the pain rushing through her.

'I had no intention of leaving you behind,' was his only comment. 'Do you have a valid passport?'

'Yes,' said Maisy. 'But why—?'

'Pack a bag. We move in twenty.'

'But—'

He gave her a brief, almost offended look. 'I'm not accustomed to explaining myself.'

To staff, added Maisy silently, biting down on a sharp retort.

Alexei registered her frustration, thinking wryly it was nothing next to his own. He had to get out of there before he did something stupid. He had overlooked momentarily who this woman was—a future employee. And he didn't bed his female staff. He left her to it, reaching for his pager as he plunged down the stairs to alert his men to the changed situation.

It took Maisy twenty minutes to bag up enough of Kostya's belongings for a week's stay. She assumed the rest of his life would come later. Her own would take considerably longer to assemble, but fortunately she still had that suitcase she had packed for France on Sunday. Only five days ago, but it felt a lifetime.

But before she took a step out that front door she was going to have a shower.

Downstairs, Alexei consulted his watch for the third time. Half an hour. It wasn't as if he wasn't used to waiting on a woman. He had yet to meet one whose 'five more minutes' meant anything less than twenty. But Maisy Edmonds wasn't in any way, shape or form a date, and he didn't have time for this.

He never dealt with the small stuff, and he could have sent someone up for her, but with his libido humming he realised he actually wanted her at his side. The sparks at least were keeping him awake and functioning.

Her bedroom door was slightly ajar. He gave it a push, half expecting to find her knee-deep in clothes. Instead he found a naked wet woman wrapped in a little white towel, with ringlets of damp hair cascading down her back.

Lust roared through him like a hot desert wind, obliterating thought.

She didn't cry out, or protest, or do any of the things an outraged woman should do in this situation—something that would make him turn around and leave her alone. She just gaped at him, clutching at the towel, her eyes growing wider, and then she actually stepped towards him.

He crossed the space between them, caught her around that surprisingly small waist and pulled her into his body, half dragging the towel off in the process. He was conscious of her making a noise as he hungrily took her mouth with his own, his tongue invading the sweetness inside. She was stiff in his arms, and he could feel her hands pushing at his biceps, but the rest of her was soft and pliant. Everything about her was everything he wanted in that moment; she was all feminine roundness and softness and warmth. He could bury himself in her and forget everything that had happened, everything that was going to happen. Sweet oblivion inside sweet Maisy.

Maisy could hardly form a coherent thought. Shock had turned to humiliation as she felt her towel shift and drop, and she was aware that at any moment she would be completely naked in a strange man's arms. This man was kissing her with a passion that went beyond expertise, as if his mouth and his tongue and his touch were desperately searching for something from her. And Maisy found something in herself was tentatively responding. The resistance melted out of her hands as she nestled closer to the source of this warmth that was spreading through her, seeking the shelter his arms offered, leaning into the strength that seemed so much a part of him. His hunger softened into something else as she began to respond.

It was almost too much. Her heartbeat was speeding out of control and his arms around her were almost too powerful, too possessive. She struggled a little, but only to drag his head back down to hers as he shifted in response, and she felt him laugh uninhibitedly against her mouth. He half lifted her and swept her up against the back of the door. It slammed with a thud, his forearm taking the brunt for her back, and Maisy felt his other big, callused hand smooth up her inner thigh. She grabbed it, muttered, 'No,' against his hair, and his mouth dropped to the pulse-point throbbing at the base of her throat. He licked her like a big cat, right there, his tongue rough and wet and hot.

Oh, Lord, thought Maisy, her body on fire. *I can't do this. I'm not ready to do this.*

'Lose the towel, Maisy,' he murmured hotly against her ear, his hands at her hips, moving around to cup her bare bottom.

'I can't,' she winced, embarrassment crawling through her.

And then it was over. It all happened in a moment. His mouth was gone, his hands were gone and she was leaning up against her bedroom door, clutching a towel to her near nakedness and staring into the eyes of a man who looked shell-shocked.

He rubbed the back of his hand over his mouth, as if removing the taste of her, and said in a low, fractured voice, 'That was inexcusable. I'm tired. I made a mistake. Forget it ever happened.'

Maisy's hazel eyes prickled. A mistake? Forget it ever happened?

Alexei knew he wasn't thinking straight. The girl in front of him was staring at him as if he was mad, and he couldn't blame her. He'd started something he couldn't finish. He'd left her high and dry, and the ache in his body wasn't going to go away any time soon.

What in the hell was he doing here? He had twelve security personnel scoping the property, a car waiting and a jet on the tarmac at Heathrow. And he, Alexei Ranaevsky, was tupping the nanny in an upstairs bedroom.

The goddamned *nanny*!

And doing a spectacularly lousy job of it.

Shoving aside the useless introspection, Alexei sized up the woman huddling against the door.

'You need to move so I can get out of here,' he directed. 'And for God's sake put some clothes on.'

Maisy flinched, but she still didn't move. She wanted desperately to be away from him, to be behind the bathroom door, to sink to the ground and wish away all her humiliation, but she knew the moment she stepped aside she might lose her chance.

She probably already had. He seemed so angry with her it was more than likely he had changed his mind. She should have shoved him off her to begin with. She should never have responded. She should have *remembered* Kostya came first.

Anais would be horrified if she knew what was going on, what had just happened—*in her own home*, just days after... Maisy felt so sick she actually thought she might throw up.

'Maisy.' He spoke her name abruptly.

'You haven't changed your mind?' she challenged, with what nerve she had left, strengthening her voice with the knowledge that Kostya came first. 'About me coming? With Kostya?'

For a moment he actually looked confused, as if she had said something completely out of left field when this was the only thing that mattered, wasn't it? Then he sighed and ran a hand over his unshaven face.

'No, I haven't changed my mind,' he muttered. 'God help me, I haven't changed my mind.'

She looked so lost for a moment something twisted inside him. He remembered her driven, *'No,'* when he had asked her to drop the towel, her hand like a trap on his when he'd sought to find the sweet wet place between her thighs.

But then why would she have left her door ajar if she hadn't wanted him to walk in?

Cynicism firmly in place, he took one last frustrated look at what he wasn't going to have and informed her, 'Get dressed. You've got five.'

It was the hardest walk Maisy had ever had to make. She hated him seeing her after what had happened—so much bare skin, as if offering herself up to him on a plate. He must have been watching her because she didn't hear her bedroom door close until after she'd shut herself in the bathroom and sunk onto the floor. Waves of humiliation rolled over her, and then she snatched her towel off and grabbed at the big fluffy bath sheet she should have been wearing. It wrapped around her like a hug, and she buried her face in its folds.

She'd been so uninhibited, so out of control. She'd felt his raw need, his naked desire, and she'd matched it with her own. Shame burned through her. This was not part of her bargain with herself and Anais. The last gift she could give her friend was a secure future for her son, and instead she had been wrapped around his godfather, seeking the comfort *she* needed, Kostya far from her mind.

It was the shock, she told herself. The grief. She would never have responded to him like that if she wasn't half out of her mind with misery and lack of sleep. But even as she formed the excuses she knew they were a lie, and it shamed her.

She had no choice. She must get up, wash her face, get dressed and go down there and face him. This volatile, unpredictable man was going to be Kostya's father to all intents and purposes. She must learn to deal with him.

Yet her fingers strayed to her swollen lips and she allowed herself a small shudder. That kiss. That *mistake*. It must never happen again.

CHAPTER THREE

THE boy, the plane…and the nanny.

No, cancel that last appellation. The red-haired sex kitten, curled up in her chair and pretending to sleep whilst he endeavoured to make sense of the figures being pumped into his email from New York. No sleep, the altitude, and now the unexpected introduction of his libido into the equation meant he was in danger of making a mistake that could cost a great many people their jobs.

He gestured to one of the attendants—a young guy named Leroy. Alexei didn't hire attractive female staff any more for his private jet. They tended to lose focus on their job.

'Leroy,' he said. 'Miss Edmonds. Move her. I don't want her in my eyeline.'

Leroy looked from the sleeping bundle that was Maisy back to his boss. Alexei knew what the man was thinking but would never say, so he added tiredly, 'She's not asleep. She's faking it.'

Maisy gritted her teeth. She had heard every word Alexei Ranaevsky had uttered since he'd sat down over an hour ago. Usually in Russian, usually brief and to the point. He hadn't addressed a single syllable to her. It was as if she had simply ceased to be. But apparently she was distracting to his eyeline.

She lifted her head as Leroy approached her. He bent down and said in a soft voice, 'Miss Edmonds—'

'I know.' Maisy gave him a resigned smile, then yawned, ruining it. She stretched and gathered up her angora travelling blanket, and climbed out of the luxurious seat. She looked pointedly at Alexei, who had removed his jacket and was propped with his feet up, scrolling through the information on the state-of-the-art laptop positioned in front of him. He didn't even acknowledge her, his amazing bone structure taut under this artificial light. He looked more tired than she felt, which was saying something.

'Put Miss Edmonds in a bed,' he said as she passed by him.

Alexei heard a faint, 'Thank you,' in that sweet, tangy voice of hers, and felt his whole body shift instinctively in her direction.

Down boy. He growled. This wasn't the time or the place to indulge his sudden craving for soft-eyed redheads. He'd had six long months of not particularly satisfying sex with Tara. Five months and twenty-nine days too long, in his opinion. Although not in Tara's. She was telling the press they were still 'good friends' two days after he broke up with her. Ironic, as he'd never had a female friend—and if he did he wouldn't choose Tara.

It was complicated. Maisy Edmonds was in his household, for now. Although she was no nanny. She'd lied to him straight up—another element to keep in mind. He had a fair idea who she was: one of Anais's crew of hangers-on. Somehow she'd inveigled her way into the house and into Kostya's life. If Leo was alive he might have vouched for her—a single word would have sufficed. But if Leo had been alive Alexei would never have met her in such fraught circumstances, leading to such a stupid indiscretion.

Which was bound to happen again.

The fierceness of her sexual response had taken even him off guard. It had turned blind need into something more exciting, edgier. It had been he who was out of control, he recognised. Whilst she had met him every inch of the way, she had also backed down fast. Meeting that resistance had saved him from a very big mistake, and possibly a costly one. Because there were always consequences.

He didn't do casual sex. And he didn't do sex full stop with-out a condom—which he wasn't carrying. He could only have her word on where she'd been. He wondered if Leo… Then he closed down that thought, because it suddenly made him very angry. An image of Maisy Edmonds in a towel, rubbing her-self against a series of men, flashed through his tired brain, firing his temper, and he swore.

It wasn't going to happen—not in the coming days and weeks anyway. The dust still had to settle on Leo's portfolio, and more importantly there was his child.

Kostya had been unexpectedly lively earlier on the trip, but now was sleeping as if the world had ended. Alexei envied him that ability to completely shut down. He imagined he had possessed it once, many aeons ago, when he was an infant. A childhood rubbed raw by neglect and strife had worn it off. He rarely slept a regular eight hours. The past few days had robbed him even of that.

With the kitten safely put to bed, he could focus on what the screen was telling him. None of it was good news. His shares in Kulcor were merely window dressing. If the company foun-dered it wouldn't show up as a blip on his financial radar, but it was Kostya's inheritance—he had to hold it. It was the least Leo would have expected of him. Family came first. However, growing up with nothing but the clothes on his back had taught Alexei to value material security. When people let you down, abandoned you, and all you had was yourself, several billion in the bank was a nice bulwark against destitution.

Leo's son would never want for anything. He would make sure of it.

A bed. Not *the* bed—not the one and only bedroom on a private jet—but *a* bed. One of three. What kind of a man had three bedrooms on a plane? Maisy smiled helplessly at her thoughts. He had a private plane. The number of bedrooms was prob-ably beside the point.

She sat down on the sumptuous bed, looking around at the

luxurious fabrics on the walls and furniture. She ran her hand over the silky bed coverings in deep purple and black. A man had definitely chosen the colour scheme, although she couldn't quite picture Alexei Ranaevsky spending much time with fabric swatches.

She could, however, imagine him on this bed, and her mind began to drift as she settled down under the luxurious covers, entertaining imagery mainly to do with him diving into bed with her. In the fantasy she didn't stop him; she was confident and even sexually aggressive. Part of her wanted to call a halt to the daydreaming—it wasn't healthy; she could never act on it. He probably wouldn't fancy her in the cold light of day… But another, darker part seized on his mouth hot on hers and his hand like a brand on her inner thigh. She shifted in the bed, irritatedly aware she was arousing herself, which only made it all worse.

She was never like this. She didn't fantasise about men to the point where she got hot and bothered. Her mind just didn't go there. Mind you, she hadn't had *time* to have a rich fantasy life, let alone an active sex life. Not with a baby. She wasn't even accustomed to air travel. She was the original stay-at-home girl. With the Kulikovs there had been several shuttles to the Paris house, but life with a new baby had pretty much shut down her opportunities to explore further afield than the Île de la Cité.

Her thoughts drifted from blue-eyed, hard-bodied Russian oligarchs to the more prosaic realities of her life. It had been impossible to leave Kostya for more than a few hours, and Anais had insisted no one had Maisy's 'way' with him. The deal had been she would have two days a week to herself, but the reality of a demanding infant had virtually turned Maisy into the mother of a newborn, with all the rigours that involved. The only normal life she had ever had was in those few months before Anais gave birth. Then they'd been girlfriends together, enjoying each other's company and all the fun opportunities London had to offer.

Leo had been home a lot then too, as Anais grew huge, and settled, hovering over her protectively, acting on her merest whim. Maisy had envied her friend that security, that devotion. Anais in turn had encouraged her to date, pushed her out through the door with a gaggle of Anais's other girlfriends into nightclubs.

For a few months she had lived like any other twenty-one-year-old girl in London. Those were the days when she'd had time to spend hours trawling clothes shops and dancing until dawn. She had met a couple of boys around her age and been in the awkward position of having to choose. Dan had worked at something in the music industry that apparently involved twiddling knobs, but he had been gentle and self-effacing and would sit up talking to her in little cafes until dawn drew her back to Lantern Square and Anais's barrage of delighted interrogation.

She had finally gone back to his flat near Earls Court and slept with him. It had seemed the right thing to do, moving the relationship along, except it hadn't quite turned out that way. She remembered lying there on his hard bed, staring at the pattern of cracks in the ceiling as Dan pushed into her virgin body, feeling self-conscious about their nakedness and wondering if she was doing something wrong. It had been quick and painful and messy, and not something she particularly wanted to repeat with him, and with that thought had came the utter certainty she had made a mistake.

She hadn't shared this with Anais—she hadn't told anybody. And a few days later, after an awkward coffee with Dan and an invitation to spend the weekend with him on a working trip, she'd ended it. The fact that he hadn't seemed too bothered had made her wonder if she was the only girl in his life.

Within weeks Anais had gone into labour, and Maisy's life as she'd begun to live it had been over. From then on, for two years, she had been the mother of a demanding baby boy.

It would have been impossible to make Alexei Ranaevsky understand the complexities of her relationship with Anais and Kostya last night. He probably would have been even less inclined to take her along. 'A friend of Anais's' sounded insubstantial—and, knowing many of Anais's girlfriends, she wouldn't have left a pot plant in their care, let alone a two-year-old.

No, *nanny* sounded sensible and professional and *useful*.

He needed a nanny, not a flighty girl with her head in a fashion magazine and her body on a beach in Ibiza. Yet deception did not sit easily with her. She wanted to be herself, not an imitation of whatever was expected of a nanny in this man's home. She hadn't even asked him if he had a partner or children. It would be shocking, given his actions last night, but not unheard of. Maisy had lived long enough in Anais's world to know adultery was a common coin and nobody blinked an eye.

What had happened tonight made no sense to her—from his perspective at least. He must have read signals into her behaviour, and she thought guiltily about the way she had visually eaten him up. She was less irresistible to him. He had been far more in control than she had. It had been he who had stopped it, owned it for a mistake.

He was clearly exhausted. The shadows under those beautiful eyes…the lines carved around his sensual mouth. Running on empty, Leo would say. Maybe she'd been available fuel, a willing female body. And she *had* been willing—shamingly willing. She had never felt that instant drench of attraction in her life. She still couldn't look at him without wanting to touch him, feel the solid heat of his body pressed up against hers. It was *wicked*.

She rolled onto her back, staring up at a ceiling starred with dozens of tiny pinpricks of light. Was this how Anais had felt about Leo? Was this like the wellspring of her friend's uninhibited passion for her husband, which had manifested itself as a longing for him whenever he was absent and a great deal of time spent in the bedroom, or the library, or on the kitchen table—much to Maisy's embarrassment as she'd come home unexpectedly one afternoon?

This was what she had been looking for, Maisy realised with a start. This passion. This excitement. This much man.

Except he was the wrong man.

Just as she was the wrong woman. The nanny.

Dawn was breaking over Naples when they hit the tarmac. Maisy had never travelled in a private jet, and the waiting limos were another shock to her system.

Alexei Ranaevsky was seriously loaded.

He was also not coming with them.

In the first limo with Kostya, Maisy gathered the courage to ask Carlo, who was travelling with them, why not.

'A chopper to Rome,' he replied briefly. 'London has held up several important meetings.'

Meaning his visit to Lantern Square. Perversely, Maisy felt a rush of anger towards both Carlo and Alexei. Kostya was not a *hold-up*. He was a little boy who had lost his parents. Surely Alexei could carve out more than an overnight flit to welcome the child?

Carlo gave her a wry look. 'Don't worry, *bella*, he'll be back. You'll see enough of him.'

Maisy stiffened at the familiarity of *bella*, and its implications. Plain enough words, but all of a sudden Maisy wondered if Alexei had spoken to Carlo, revealed what had occurred. It was too crass to bear thinking about, but Maisy's hands made fists in her lap and her whole body was on red alert.

She averted her face to the window and didn't say another word.

So this was where he lived.

The sixteenth-century exterior of Villa Vista Mare had not hinted at its sleek interior: soaring ceilings, glass everywhere, and blinding white surfaces. It was like stepping into the future. Maisy was accustomed to the shabby Georgian chic at

Lantern Square and the pretty comfort of the Kulikovs' other residence on the Île de la Cité in Paris. This sort of cutting-edge modernity and the money it took to fuel it was startling, and also troubling. Kostya's life was going to be here now. It screamed style and money and glamour. It didn't hold you in its arms and murmur 'home'.

Seven days later she was doing her best to install some of Lantern Square into Kostya's surroundings. She couldn't fault the nursery. Not unexpectedly, it was over the top. Alexei clearly believed the advent of a child into his life called for lots of *stuff*. The life-size pony on rockers was perhaps the worst of it. A sleigh for a bed was inspired. Over the week she had shifted the worst out and created a softer space.

Kostya was universally loved by the household; Maria the housekeeper, a handsome woman in her middle fifties, doted on him. But every morning Maisy woke with the expectation that today would be the day Alexei Ranaevsky would put in an appearance, and every morning she was disappointed. She couldn't make sense of his behaviour. He had spoken of his responsibility for Kostya, yet his actions spoke volumes as to where he saw Kostya in his life.

There was a room for the nanny off the nursery. It was utilitarian, with a view of the courtyard wall. Maisy tried not to spend any time in there other than to sleep, and she slept a lot. Alexei had organised a night nurse to be on duty, which meant she could sleep through the night for the first time since Kostya had been born. Six nights of uninterrupted sleep. She felt a hundred years younger.

Every day she took Kostya down to the beach in the morning, and read books on the terrace during the afternoon whilst he took his nap. In the evenings she would have liked to eat with Maria, but the housekeeper usually left at seven, after providing a solo meal. The rest of the skeleton staff seemed paid to be invisible. It was as if she was living in a palatial hotel all by herself.

On the seventh day she asked Maria if she might have a car to take down into the town. She had noticed a converted stable in the grounds securing seven sleek luxury vehicles.

'I don't want anything fancy,' she hastened to add. 'Just some beat-up thing I can motor about in.'

Maria laughed at her. 'You can borrow mine, Maisy. It's insured, and there's a child's seat in the back. I use it for my granddaughter.'

Maisy recognised that she was feeling a wild pleasure at the thought of getting out of the villa out of proportion to the lure of shops and other people. She ran upstairs and shimmied out of her T-shirt and shorts, replacing them with a green-and-pink floral sundress she had bought for her aborted trip to Paris. It was modest in the neckline, protecting her décolletage from the harsh sunshine, and fell just above her knees, but was virtually backless. She whipped her hair out of its ponytail and shook out her curls, solving that problem.

She got Kostya ready and strapped him into the car, giving Maria an enthusiastic wave as she rolled out of the courtyard and took off up the dusty road towards the highway that would take her down the hairpin bends and dips of the road into Ravello.

She had specific chores to undertake: organise funds from her English bank account, purchase a sturdier hat to protect Kostya from the fiery Italian sun, and stock up on trashy paperbacks. But it was impossible not to get sidetracked by the beauty of the old town.

Crossing the road after purchasing *gelato* for herself and Kostya, she spotted a beauty therapist's. The warm breeze caressed her bare legs and reminded her she was in desperate need of a wax. With Kostya sucking on his ice and occupied with a box of toys, she was able to deal with her legs *and* have her hair trimmed and blow-dried. Feeling infinitely more attractive than she had going in, Maisy strapped Kostya back into his pushchair and headed for the gardens she had spotted at the other end of the road.

Several cars slowed down, passing her, and a group of youths called out in Italian to her. She didn't understand a word but it was fairly clear it was appreciative. Maisy shook her head in disbelief. A pretty dress and 'new' hair and suddenly she was on display.

'Don't you grow up to be so silly, Kostya,' she said, ruffling the top of his fair head.

A screeching of tyres made her look up. A low-slung sports car was humming alongside the kerb. Maisy froze.

'Get in the car.'

Maisy released a deep breath, unaware she had been holding it. *Alexei.*

He was leaning over the steering wheel, his cobalt eyes hidden behind razor-sharp sunglasses. He looked what he was: cool, ruthless, very male.

She needed to handle this with the same cool. It was important not to appear eager or pleased or even furious that it had taken him seven days—*seven days*—to put in an appearance. It wasn't easy when any woman in her right mind would have leapt in that car with him without a second thought.

She glanced ahead at the gardens and then, deciding, put the brake on the pushchair and crossed the few steps to the kerb, leaning in.

'We're going to the gardens. I promised Kostya.'

She turned her back on his incredulous face, kicked off the brake and kept moving, making a beeline for the gates.

Alexei slotted the car into a space overlooking the sea and took off after Maisy on foot. When Maria had casually told him Maisy had just walked out of the villa and taken the boy with her he'd been annoyed his security team hadn't been alerted. The further information that she had taken Maria's old Audi had infuriated him. Those hairpin bends were suicidal if you didn't know them. But it was the sight of her in a flowery dress, with her arms and legs bare and all those pre–Raphaelite curls flowing down her back, being cat-called and ogled by Italian males that had sent him over the top.

Maisy wasn't sure if he would drive away and leave them alone, or come after them. What she didn't expect was for him to lay a hand on her elbow and wrench her almost off her feet. He whisked her around as if she were a doll. She had forgotten how big he was. The breadth of his shoulders and his musculature were outlined by the expensive weave of an olive T-shirt. Held up against him, Maisy felt warmth sweeping up into her cheeks, his proximity having the same upending effect on her senses it had had in London.

'What in the *hell* do you think you're doing?' he blistered at her.

The sunglasses meant she couldn't see his eyes, but she could feel them nevertheless—boring into her.

'Going into the gardens,' she answered, trying to pull her arm free. But he had a firm grip. 'For goodness' sake, let me go. I don't understand why you're so angry.'

Alexei took in her wide hazel eyes and soft mouth, the colour in her cheeks. She was a time bomb waiting to go off. He couldn't have this much woman living under his roof. He'd end up giving her anything she asked for.

She made a soft distressed sound as his hand instinctively tightened and he released her immediately, shocked by his own conduct. He had imagined—*imagined*—he could deal with her in a short interview at the house. Confront her with his investigator's report, set out the terms for her remaining with Kostya until he settled, and then ignore her. He was doing a good job of ignoring her. For six days and seven nights. Long nights—except for the sixteen hours he had slept under the effect of a sedative.

He wasn't unaccustomed to periods of time without a woman in his bed. There was something rejuvenating about the spread of a cool, empty king-size bed. But Maisy Edmonds had been there every night in his waking dreams, with her wild red curls and her lush, eminently squeezable bottom, and the spicy taste of her still tingling in his mouth. He hadn't misremembered her mouth—it *was* sweet and pink. The places he had imagined that mouth had been… To see it now, unmarked by lipstick, soft and innocent-looking, he felt like a sex-crazed brute.

'Leave my Maisy alone!' stated Kostya, standing up in his pushchair. He had managed to unclip his belt, and this held Maisy's amazed attention, whilst Alexei, deeply shaken by his reaction, faced her little protector with a tad more subtlety.

He instantly dropped down to Kostya's height. 'I didn't mean to upset Maisy. I'm Maisy's friend too. I came to bring you both home.'

'Don't want to go home. Want to be on holiday.'

'The villa *is* holiday,' explained Maisy, still looking at Alexei uneasily, as if he was liable to spring at her.

Alexei released his breath with a hiss and straightened up, extending his arms to Kostya. 'Come on, little man. How about I carry you for a bit?'

Kostya looked up at Maisy, and after a hesitation she nodded encouragingly, holding her breath as Alexei lifted the little boy into his arms. For a minute it seemed he might protest, but Alexei held him confidently, and Maisy saw the moment the little body relaxed into the man's shoulder.

It gave her a chance to observe him more closely. He was wearing jeans and they clung to him like a second skin. They also made him look younger, and it occurred to Maisy for the first time he was really only a few years older than she was. He couldn't be more than thirty and look at the life he led, the power he wielded, the level of sophistication he wore so casually. Maisy suddenly felt hopelessly out of her depth—and she was—but she had Kostya's wellbeing to fight for, and that gave her the added push she needed.

And the fact remained he had been gone for an entire week.

'Where have you been for the last seven days?' The words were out of her mouth before discretion could check her tongue.

He shrugged. 'What does it matter? I'm here now.'

He was here now. Maisy simmered on that for a few minutes as they resumed their stroll. She leaned into the pushchair that felt light as a feather now Kostya wasn't in it.

'How long will you stay?' she asked evenly, as if it were not the most important question.

'I've factored in three days.' He announced it with an air of magnanimity that stole Maisy's breath away.

Three days! She studied the man beside her. She was aware people were watching them, women were watching *him*. A couple of beautiful Italian girls perhaps her own age swung past them, sweeping Alexei's length with unabashed sexual speculation. Maisy blushed for him. Alexei, however, seemed completely unaware of anyone but herself and Kostya. In fact his focus was a little intimidating.

'Three days isn't very long,' she ventured quietly, carefully.

'It's all I have.' His tone was a warning to cease questioning him, to keep her mouth shut. She remembered his statement— *'I don't explain my actions.'* Certainly not to the nanny, she thought wryly.

'Explain to me why you borrowed Maria's car and made this very dangerous little trip into town,' he said in a quiet undertone clearly used to avoid disturbing Kostya.

He had pushed the sunglasses back through his hair revealing those incredible eyes that were every bit as intense as she remembered.

'It wasn't dangerous,' she replied, copying his neutral tone. 'I'm a good driver and I'm careful.' Then the truth surfaced and she made a frustrated sound. 'You try being cooped up in one place for a full seven days.'

He smiled slowly, knowingly. 'You were bored, *dushka*?'

Maisy was startled by the smile, the sudden intimacy of his tone. She shook it off with the suspicion he was probably like this with all women under thirty, unthinkingly working them up with throwaway charisma.

'Not bored, exactly,' she said uncertainly, wondering how honest she should be.

Your house is full of people who don't talk to me; Maria and the night nurse have taken over many of the usual calls on my time; I'm only twenty-three and I feel like I've been walled up alive some days.

'I just wanted to look around, get my bearings.'

'Yes, I saw you getting your bearings on the street. Half the male population of Ravello is going to be on the villa's doorstep.'

He spoke casually, but there was an edge in his voice.

'It's not my fault if Italian men are appreciative of women,' she replied stiffly. 'I didn't invite it.'

'That dress invites it.' His tone remained casual, but Maisy heard the censure and stiffened.

'Are you suggesting I'm trying to pick up?' she challenged.

Alexei's expression was taut, hinting at inner tensions she couldn't guess at. 'I'm Kostya's guardian,' he enunciated plainly. 'I expect you to behave like a lady and not flaunt yourself.'

Maisy didn't know what to say. In what way had she flaunted herself? What was wrong with coming into town for the day? What was wrong with her dress? All of a sudden the warmth and freedom of the day dwindled down to a cluster of doubts, and Maisy tugged self-consciously on her skirt. She couldn't help flashing back to herself in a towel, stunned by his presence in her room. Was that the impression he had of her? A woman who displayed herself to strange men for sex? She cringed at the thought.

The truth wasn't much better, and it wasn't fair. It was him. It was because of him she had responded so uninhibitedly. But how could she explain that to him without making even more of a fool of herself?

Kostya had slumped over Alexei's shoulder, taking in the view from this new height. He looked so comfortable up there Maisy only felt worse.

She had to rid herself of this stupid infatuation. It wasn't fair to Kostya, and it wasn't fair to her.

'You've gone very quiet,' Alexei said in a neutral voice.

'I'm sorry. I wasn't aware I was supposed to entertain you. I wouldn't want to be accused of flaunting myself.' Where had that bitter tone come from? She bit her tongue.

Alexei's eyes swept her body in a way that was disturbingly intimate, met her stormy eyes. 'You can have a social life here, Maisy. I just don't want you bringing men back to the villa.'

Maisy almost choked, forced to defend herself. 'What men? The only men I've seen for the past week have been in uniforms, and they barely give me the time of day!'

'Hence your little day out.' He spoke so quietly, so reasonably, Maisy could have hit him.

She stopped on the path, aware there were other people around and that Kostya, however young, shouldn't be overhearing this conversation. 'I think you've made it clear how low your opinion of me can go. I don't think I should have to defend myself when I've done nothing wrong.'

Alexei instantly felt like a jerk. He knew he was being tough on her, but she provoked him. She was so lovely even a sackcloth wouldn't stop men looking at her, and why it bothered him so much he was struggling to understand.

Because you want her, and if it backfires you're stuck with her, a cool, cynical voice intervened.

The child heavy in his arms was a reminder of how careful he had to be.

'I think we should go back,' he said gruffly. 'The boy has fallen asleep.'

Maisy didn't reply. She just jerked the lightweight pushchair around and headed back up the path ahead of him.

It occurred to him she was acting like a girlfriend, not the nanny. And he didn't have any experience of girlfriends.

Alexei took them back to the villa in his high-speed toy at a reasonable pace, handling the bends with such care and confidence Maisy realised he might have a point about the danger. Maria's Audi would be returned to her by a despatched member of staff.

There was a taut, tense silence in the car that was tying Maisy's stomach in knots.

She took a deep breath and examined his hard, uncompromising profile as he negotiated the road. An innocent trip into town had been turned into a man-trawling exercise on her part. He was clearly ready to believe the worst of her because it would make it easier for him to get rid of her when the time came.

Whatever I do, she thought a little desperately, *it won't be enough because he's decided I'm a party girl*. Which was so ludicrous she snorted.

His attention snapped to her. 'What is it?'

Maisy checked over her shoulder. Kostya's head was hanging; he was still deeply asleep.

She gave Alexei her best impression of Anais-like insouciance. 'I was just thinking, if all the men in Ravello are hot for me I'm going to need some evenings off to accommodate them. How about Fridays and Saturdays?'

It was a stupid thing to do, but he was *so* self-righteous. She wanted to show him how silly all his preconceptions of her actually were. Instead, the moment the words were out of her mouth she knew she had made a mistake.

The car shifted down a gear, slowed, came to a soft standstill on the side of the road. Alexei unsnapped his safety belt, glancing into the backseat at the slumbering infant. Maisy shrank back against the door, suddenly wary of what she'd stirred up.

'Wh—what are you doing?' she stammered.

'I need to make a call,' he informed her, head averted, scissoring the door open and closed.

Lacing his hands behind his neck, Alexei walked out his frustration along the verge, taking a few deep breaths. She was a very young, very provocative woman. She was taunting him because he'd offended her. She didn't mean to push his buttons. But she had.

He couldn't drive safely until he'd worked this through.

All the men in Ravello. He'd brought it up. He'd put the words into her mouth. He'd put the thoughts into her head. Maisy was clearly no more promiscuous than he was. Yet…images he'd never be free of flashed like a viewfinder through his mind. His mother's clients—sordid, terrifying for the child he had been. He let them flicker, then shut them off with abrupt practised closure, glancing back at the car. He could see her head bent, the gleam of all those fiery ringlets. He took a breath. This was Maisy—this was different. There was nothing more natural than his desire to take her to bed.

Maisy sat drowning in the sudden silence. She watched him in the rear-vision mirror as he walked slowly away from the car. Even through her shot nerves she registered his back view was every bit as scrumptious as the front, and he had an amazing taut behind.

She buried her hot face in her hands. *Me and my mouth,* she cursed. *What was I thinking? What am I doing? It was a joke—a silly joke. But of course he doesn't do jokes. This is all getting completely out of hand.*

She heard a click and felt the shift of weight in the car, dragging her hands away too late to find him beside her, watching her with the oddest expression. It was too late to hide her embarrassment.

Unsophisticated, foot-in-mouth Maisy.

'That didn't take long,' she blurted out, sounding uncomfortably breathless.

He was watching her and there was real, undisguised heat in his eyes. Maisy's breathing hitched and sped up. The buzzing atmosphere she recognised from her room was in the car. She had never felt anything like it, and with it came the memory of the feel of his mouth sliding over hers, the sheer force of his lust. You couldn't dress it up as anything else—they barely knew one another, and she had been with him all the way. Why wouldn't he think she would do it again?

'I decided I didn't need to make the call.' A smile sat tight on his lips as he turned over the quiet engine. 'Maybe you should reconsider all the men in Ravello, Maisy. I have a feeling you're going to be pretty busy.'

'With Kostya?' said Maisy by rote, her mouth dry, her throat closed.

'No.' He swung the sports car fluidly back onto the highway and accelerated ever so slightly, so that the breath leapt from her body. 'That would be with me.'

CHAPTER FOUR

By the time they drew into the courtyard she was a mass of nerves, but Alexei, in contrast, seemed completely energised. He already had Kostya out of his child's seat and was carrying him and the pushchair inside with the casual assurance that he would keep the boy with him for the rest of the afternoon—leaving Maisy to fumble with her shopping bag, feeling utterly swamped.

So much for looking after him. She was left with the shopping.

She could hardly credit what had happened. He had to be joking. He couldn't possibly be suggesting what it sounded like he was suggesting. She chased his words around her head as she went through the motions of decanting her purchases onto her bed and taking a shower in the modest *en suite* bathroom to freshen up. She was so distracted she almost doused her brand-new hair, just dodging the water stream in time.

This whole sexual attraction thing was inappropriate and dangerous. Alexei was like that car of his—high-powered. Things could veer out of control if she didn't handle him properly. She needed to tone it down, deflect him in some way. The problem was deep down she liked his approval—she liked that spark he got in his eyes. The woman in her did a slow burn every time he so much as looked in her direction.

Pulling on yoga pants and a long T-shirt, she told herself these clothes would firmly put the kybosh on any inclinations he had in her direction. Except, lingering in front of the mirror, she knew she was kidding herself. Deep down she wanted what she'd had in her room in London. She wanted him to look at her and lose control again. At the same time the idea terrified her, because it would involve tipping into a level of sexual intimacy she didn't know if she was ready for. A solitary horrible experience had not encouraged her in any way to repeat it, even if she had the opportunity. But for a week now in her darkest thoughts he had been there, lifting her, his mouth on her, the heat of his body being accepted into hers.

Her reflection in the mirror taunted her. Her skin felt tight, hot and her eyes as dark as she'd ever seen them, the pupils enlarged. Her body was giving her messages she was finding difficult to ignore.

Frustrated with herself, Maisy stripped and pulled on a soft knit top and her favourite jeans instead. They weren't obvious but they clung in all the right places. She told herself there was nothing wrong with enjoying a little male attention. She just needed to keep everything within bounds.

She could hear Kostya before she reached him. Alexei was sprawled on the floor with him in the entertainment room. Maisy hesitated, watching them. They were building blocks, and every time Alexei got eight up Kostya would knock them down, shrieking with glee. *Within bounds?* a dry little voice murmured in her head. *And whose bounds would they be, Maisy, his or yours?*

Alexei's head came up and she knew who had won.

'I can't win,' he said, his dark voice full of rich amusement. 'He's clearly experienced in demolition. I might employ him.'

Maisy took one step and then another into the room. She had not seen him so relaxed before and it made a spectacular sight.

Alexei made a round trip of Maisy whilst Kostya crawled about collecting his blocks. The scoop-necked knit top clung gently to the round shape of her full breasts and flared out over her hips. She was shaped like an hourglass—something he hadn't fully appreciated until this moment. If his hands were around that little waist of hers he was sure his fingers would meet. The jeans were like a second skin, tapering over her slender calves to her small feet.

Maisy exuded a soft femininity that had the testosterone pounding through him, obliterating any sensible thought he might have had about putting the lid on this attraction. Her curves, he recognised in a flash of clarity, made a nightmare of every sharp hipbone he had ever cut himself on.

Only one thought was pumping through his brain: where had this woman been all his life? His mouth was dry by the time she crouched down and brushed the curls from Kostya's eyes.

'He needs a haircut.' His voice was thick, darkened by the sexual impulses thrumming through his blood.

Her mouth tensed. He loved that she didn't wear lipstick. 'Not yet.'

'I'll get a barber in.'

'No.' A little frown line creased between her brows.

'Are you going to fight me on everything, Maisy?'

'If I have to.'

A very blatant image of Maisy naked, on top of him, assaulted his senses, and all Alexei could do about it was smile at her, wondering what magic words were going to break down whatever defences she had in place.

Maisy was making sure she looked him in the eye. He needed to understand when it came to Kostya she wouldn't let him steamroll her. But then he smiled that lazy big cat smile that made her tingle down to her toes and suspect they weren't talking about Kostya at all. She did her best to ignore the tingling.

'I don't think now is a good time for haircuts.'

Alexei sat up, the movement so abrupt Maisy almost jumped. He was sitting so close to where she was hunkered down she could have reached out and brushed the back of her hand along his lightly bristled jaw. She blushed at the thought.

'I spoke to a child psychologist on Monday,' he responded.

Right. Child psychologist. Good. Maisy moistened her lips. 'Maybe we can talk about it later,' she said jerkily, trying not to read too much into his close proximity. 'Kostya might be little but he has big ears.' She struggled to inject some normality into her voice, which seemed to have dropped an octave. 'Besides, it's the three Bs: bathtime, booktime, bedtime.'

Alexei could have punched the air in a victory salute. She was feeling him: the pink in her cheeks, the glitter in those cinnamon eyes. She was just a little nervous. Or it could be anticipation. He had no idea. She wasn't putting out obvious 'come and get me' signals, just little indicators she couldn't control.

'I can do that,' he replied, surging to his feet. Time to get this train on the tracks. He scooped up Kostya, who shrieked with excitement.

'No, no, you'll overstimulate him.' Maisy sighed as she clambered to her feet. She was feeling distinctly unlike herself. Her skin was prickling with awareness and she couldn't seem to get in enough air. Instinctively she stumbled back to avoid brushing against Alexei as he moved with Kostya, shoving her hands in her jeans' back pockets to disguise their trembling.

Overstimulation *was* in the air, Alexei reflected ruefully, looking down at her. Damn, she was sexy. He tried not to let his gaze drift south of her pretty mouth. It was very uncool. But he was enjoying that too—the sheer craziness of what was going on.

He followed her upstairs to the nursery, admiring the swing of her round, shapely bottom, knowing absolutely he was going to end tonight with his hands right there and Maisy's glorious red-gold ringlets spread over his pillow. The certainty stayed with him as he went through the bedtime routine. Maisy kept taking peeks at him when she thought he wasn't watching. He could read women's sexual arousal and he could feel Maisy's deep down to his bones. She just needed a little gentle handling and direction.

'Will you have dinner with me?' he said as Maisy grappled

with Kostya's nappy, and she gave him a wry look. Her nervousness had evaporated under the stress of managing a two-year-old and she was getting mouthy with him. He liked that too.

'Is that an excuse to get out of here whilst the going's good?'

'I can *handle* a nappy, Maisy.'

'The question is, will you in the future? Or are you going to hire a dozen people to do the job for you?'

The criticism went home. Maisy observed his slight tensing and was glad. It showed he did have an understanding of what Kostya needed. The fact that he was here now, helping her, had gone a long way to calming her fears. She had also managed not to touch him, ogle him, or say anything that could be misconstrued. In fact, she had behaved like a completely sexless plant.

Perfect.

'Dinner, Maisy?' he repeated.

'I usually eat in the dining room at seven,' she said. 'Will you join me then?'

Alexei dealt her a look of combined disbelief and complete amusement.

'I think, *dushka*, we can do better than that.'

Dinner.

Maisy covered her hot face with her hands. She was going to sleep with him. Maybe. It was good to be clear about these things. She wouldn't think about next week or the month after or the year after that. She would just go for it and damn the consequences. Other women did it all the time.

She was a modern girl. She knew what was on offer.

She was kidding herself.

Maisy groaned and flopped onto her bed. Beside her lay the two outfits she couldn't decide between. Her one cocktail dress looked too formal and insubstantial, and clearly said, *Take me now. I'm not even wearing a bra.* Definitely not suitable.

The strapless white silk frock was really for the daytime,

but she could dress it up with a necklace, some make-up, and do something fancy with her hair. The bodice was boned and did the work of a bra. Just about.

In the end she made up her eyes and mouth to stand in for the simplicity of her dress and clasped a gold filigree necklace around her neck. She used a clip to twist up her hair so that it toppled in disarray, the tips kissing the curve of her shoulder-blades. She slid her feet into a pair of very high silver heels and used the sliding doors to step out into the courtyard so as not to disturb Kostya.

She climbed the back stairs to the kitchen, feeling a little like Cinderella gearing up for the ball and going in the back way.

'Maisy, *bella figura*!' Maria exclaimed in Italian when she came into the kitchen, dusting off her floury hands and leaving the bread she was kneading to come and encircle Maisy, smiling broadly.

'Dinner with the boss, eh?' Maria folded her arms, shaking her head.

'To talk about Kostya,' Maisy answered primly.

The older woman gave her an old-fashioned look. 'He's a good boy,' observed Maria. 'But all these parties, these women.' She threw her hands up expressively.

Parties? *Women?* Maisy just knew she didn't want to hear any of this. Yet when Maria sighed and went back to kneading the bread she wanted to scream, *And?*

Maria's raisin-brown eyes slanted sideways at Maisy. 'What he needs is a good girl who can cook, raise the *bambinos* and keep him happy in the bed, yes?'

Maisy didn't know where to look. Cook, clean and heat up the sheets… Oh, and don't forget the baby-making factory. No, thank you.

'He might have learned the English, and he has the houses in Miami and New York, but he's European.' Maria leaned her floury forearms on the board and fixed Maisy with a steely determination at odds with her short, round little body. 'The

Russian men—they're like the Italians. They are traditional. Oh, times have moved on, and Alexei is what they say—*a modern guy*—but when he settles down…'

Maria straightened up with a sigh and wiped her hands.

'He doesn't particularly strike me as being ready to settle down just yet,' Maisy muttered, wishing they weren't having this conversation so close to her sitting down to dinner with him in a strapless dress.

'If you leave it to the men they'll *never* be ready,' said Maria. 'They always need the little nudge.'

Alexei would need some heavy earth moving equipment and possibly a natural disaster to shift him out of bachelor status, Maisy thought ruefully. He didn't strike her at all as the marrying type.

'You must be careful, Maisy,' said the older woman, her eyes settling on Maisy's flushed décolletage. 'He is the real man, and he will chase you, and you're a nice girl.'

The real man. That he was, thought Maisy, giving her bodice an upward tug in an effort to reinstate the 'nice girl'. Preoccupied, she made her way into the dining room. Alexei wasn't there, but one of his suits was waiting for her. Maisy recognised him as Andrei, the young man who had driven her here on the first day. He was friendly towards her in a way nobody except Maria had been since her arrival and, feeling nervous, she instantly engaged him in conversation about his day as she accompanied him upstairs and onto the roof terrace.

Alexei heard her voice before he saw her, and when she emerged he made the immediate decision never to send another man to fetch Maisy. In future he would undertake that task himself.

She was wearing some sort of frock, but it was difficult to register that when she moved, because the killer heels made her sway and he was pretty sure there was nothing between Maisy and that dress but air. The neckline was relatively modest—she wasn't spilling out of it, but the shape of her gave the impression she was. It was a dress designed to make a man think about what was poured into it. He was already planning how to take her out of it.

Maisy felt like a princess as he advanced towards her. Behind him there was a round table dressed in white and crystal, and there he was, in dark formal trousers and an expensive white shirt open at the neck to reveal the tanned strong column of his throat.

This wasn't a considered discussion about Kostya's future. This was a date.

'You always make me wait, Maisy.'

She looked up at him without understanding.

Up close, he saw she'd made a mystery of her cinnamon eyes and her lush mouth was a deep pink. There was a faint scent of exotic flowers clinging to her skin. She'd made an effort to be beautiful for him, he acknowledged. It meant *he* had to make an effort and not ravish her on the table before the first course.

He seated her and sat down across from her.

'You look beautiful, Maisy.'

She gave him a wry look. It wasn't the reaction he had been after.

'Do you always dine here, up on the rooftop?'

'Occasionally, when the mood strikes.'

He lifted the champagne and decanted some into a flute glass for her and then poured his own. Maisy watched the pale bubbles surge.

'It's so lovely,' she said, gazing around. 'I would eat up here all the time if I could. Is Maria preparing the meal?'

'I left that to the chef, *dushka*.' He looked faintly curious, as if her questions were not quite what he was expecting.

'She didn't mention it, that's all, and the kitchen was very quiet.'

'What were you doing in the kitchen?'

'Talking to Maria.'

Alexei gave her an odd look. 'Then you were talking to Andrei?'

She nodded. 'I didn't know you had a chef. Maria's been

making all my meals. She's a wonderful cook. I'm sure I'll put on ten pounds whilst I'm here if I don't start running again. Why are you staring at me? What I have said?'

'I hadn't realised you were so tight with the housekeeper,' was all he observed, sipping from his glass.

'She's been incredible with Kostya, and he's really taken to her.'

Alexei merely inclined his head, and suddenly Maisy understood the man sitting across from her didn't really care about any of this. He wasn't listening to her. He was *watching* her. He never actually looked directly at her breasts, but Maisy knew that he was *seeing* them because they had tightened, and suddenly the boning in her dress didn't feel anywhere near substantial enough.

Men didn't make a habit of looking at her like this. Especially men sitting across from her, pouring her champagne and looking as if they'd stepped out of a style magazine.

'Let's talk about Kostya,' she said, her high voice betraying a sudden rush of nerves.

'Drink your champagne, Maisy. You haven't touched a drop.'

Automatically she lifted the glass to her lips and took a sip. It tasted divine. She took another sip and sucked some of it off her lip. Premier champagne and pink shimmer lipstick—perhaps not the perfect combination.

Alexei watched her lip plump out, all wet and shiny from her tongue and the champagne. He would lick her there, later on, and then he would lick her further down, where she would also be plump and wet and wanting. He shifted in his chair as his body stirred to life.

Maisy put her glass down with a bump and he noticed her hands were trembling a little. Which was good. Hell, his weren't exactly steady. He lifted his eyes to hers, but instead of desire he saw a little worry line of concern drawing her lovely dark brows together.

'We really need to talk about Kostya,' she insisted a little more firmly.

Alexei made a frustrated but resigned sound in the back of his throat. 'Fine. We talk.'

Maisy folded her hands in her lap. She looked prim and proper—and that, he discovered, revved him up too.

'Do you intend for Kostya to live here in Ravello?'

As enquiries went it was pretty innocuous and reasonable, yet it was one Alexei knew he wouldn't answer in any other circumstances. He was so accustomed to guarding his privacy it had become habit never to respond to questions. Refusing to answer, however, wasn't conducive to persuading Maisy out of that dress, so he settled for neutral. '*Nyet.* Villa Vista Mare is only one of my homes.'

Maisy experienced a sinking feeling. 'How many do you have?'

'Seven,' he said briefly, as if it were of no import.

'Seven?' she repeated. 'What on earth do you need seven homes for?'

'Convenience,' he said after a pause.

At that moment a waiter appeared with their entrée—crab bisque—and Maisy smiled at him and waited as she was served.

Alexei wondered a little testily if she showered those smiles on every male she met except him.

'Does that mean Kostya will be travelling the world with you, to these homes?'

'*Da.*'

Maisy sighed deeply, looking past him into the flickering darkness, saying almost to herself, 'How is this going to work?'

Alexei gestured to her plate. 'Eat, Maisy. Worry later.'

She nibbled on some crab meat and finally gave him the full impact of her smile. 'It tastes of the sea,' she imparted, as if this were a wonder.

'It should,' he replied, enjoying her reaction. 'It came out of it this afternoon.'

The main course received the same enthusiasm and he watched her eat, itself a rare event. Most of the women he sat down at a table with picked their way around a plate and drank like fish. Maisy hardly touched her champagne, but cleaned up her plate.

'I've spoken to a child psychologist, as I told you earlier,' said Alexei as their plates were cleared. 'He informs me Kostya needs to feel secure here before he's told about his parents.'

'I agree completely.'

Her cheeks were flushed now—a combination of the spices in the main dish and her single half glass of champagne. Alexei knew they had to get this thorny question of Kostya's welfare sorted before he could dance with her and feed her *gelato* and watch her lick it off the spoon, and then off his tongue. He also had to get his body under control before he stood up.

'I'm dreading it,' she confessed.

He experienced a measure of guilt for his lascivious thoughts. He needed to focus on this. It mattered.

'He hasn't asked for his parents?' he said slowly.

Maisy folded her napkin. 'No.'

There was a long silence. He was clearly waiting for an explanation, but Maisy didn't know where to start without being disloyal to Anais.

For once he didn't push her, and Maisy heard herself saying, 'I don't know how it is in Russia, but often in England in high-flying families the children can be overlooked.'

Alexei went very still. 'You're telling me Leo was a neglectful parent?'

Maisy suddenly felt uncomfortable, realising she had stepped unwarily into dangerous territory. She wasn't the only person at the table protective of the Kulikovs' memory. Alexei wasn't going to like what she had to say.

'It depends on your definition of *neglect*.' She decided to talk to her plate. It seemed the easiest thing to do. 'He was a busy man—you know that. He wasn't always around.'

'Kostya is an infant,' Alexei said with some assurance. 'It's natural his mother would be his primary caregiver.'

'Anais had some difficulties.' Maisy released the breath

she had been holding. 'She was very young—only twenty-one when she had him. She wasn't particularly close to her own mother. It's hard to explain. Anais didn't spend a lot of time with Kostya.'

There—she'd said it. It was out there. She looked up to find Alexei was staring at her, and it wasn't a look she was accustomed to from him.

'What sort of concoction is this, Maisy? You're trying to make me believe Leo Kulikov wasn't a good father?'

'It's not a concoction, and I'm not saying they were bad people,' she insisted. 'I'm just trying to make you understand what's going on in Kostya's little head.'

'I don't need you for that, *dushka*, I've got a child psychologist who will deal with that problem. What I'm more interested in is why you're so keen to make me think the worst.'

'I'm not,' Maisy protested. 'You wanted to know—' She broke off, upset by the contempt she could see forming in his eyes.

'I know how much Leo loved his boy,' said Alexei, in a voice that brooked no argument.

Maisy pushed the remainder of her plate away. 'I'm not hungry any more,' she said in a low voice.

Alexei leaned towards her. 'Listen to me, Maisy. I don't want to hear these stories. They don't do you any credit. I wasn't going to bring this up with you, but I've got some questions about your background I'd like cleared up before we go any further.'

'My background?' She hated the nervous tremor in her voice. It made her sound guilty of something.

'Daughter of an unemployed single mother, yet privately educated, and you'd never held down a job until you appeared in the Kulikov household two years ago.' He wielded the facts as if they were accusations.

Maisy flinched from them. He'd brought back so many memories she had hoped to leave behind for ever. She didn't want them here tonight on this Italian rooftop. She wanted to

be the woman she was in the process of becoming. She wanted
him to be the man she had imagined him to be.

All of a sudden she felt the past was very close to the surface.

'How did you find out all that?' she asked, gathering herself together.

'It's my business to know. What? Did you think I'd just let
you in the door without a background check? Give me a break.'

'You could have asked me,' she said, with no little dignity.

'Yes, but would I believe you,' he replied silkily.

The unfairness of his accusation hurt. 'Probably not. You
seem to think I'm a liar, but to what purpose I have no idea.'

He was looking at her as if she had done something unfor-
givable—as if she'd crawled out from under a rock somewhere.
It would have been easier to make up some story, she realised
sadly, tell him the same lies everybody else had expected from
her: Leo and Anais were a super couple, with a super life and a
super baby. But the truth was—like everyone—they had been
flawed, and because they'd been larger than life their flaws
had enlarged accordingly.

'Tell me,' said Alexei with deceptive calm, 'why do you
think I invited you to have dinner with me tonight?'

Maisy knew she was walking into a trap. She would answer
and he would say something clever and she would look a bigger fool. So she didn't say anything. She stared endlessly at
her half-empty champagne glass as the seconds ticked by.

'Did you think, Maisy, we were going to talk about your
employment contract? With you in your strapless frock and
me pouring you champagne?'

Don't say it, she willed him. *Please don't say it.*

'Or did you think I was going to take you to bed and keep
you in the style to which you've become accustomed?'

His words stripped her of cover. She had nowhere to hide
from them because it was true. She had wanted to go to bed
with him. She had worn her best dress and her laciest knickers. She had drunk some of the champagne for Dutch courage.

Kostya's future had come second to her desire to draw Alexei to her.

For the first time she had put the little boy second and herself first, and now she was going to pay for it. He'd set her up. She wasn't fit to look after the needs of a young child. She was a sex-crazed bimbo.

Swallowing hard, she lifted guilty eyes to meet his icy scorn. Her dignity lay in shreds around her. She felt the same way she had when huddled behind the bathroom door at Lantern Square. He *did* this to her.

'Are you going to send me away?' she asked hollowly.

Their eyes locked.

'Don't be ridiculous.'

There was a fraught silence.

Alexei suddenly wanted to smash the last five minutes and go back to where they'd been before. She was looking at him like a deer caught in the headlights—that same lost look he remembered from London. It made him want to gather her up and shelter her from the harsher realities of life, including his own. But she'd pushed all his buttons with that crack about Leo. It was absurd and it was wrong, he told himself.

'Kostya needs you.'

Maisy frowned. He said it as if the idea was distasteful to him. As if she was everything he said she was. It gave her the nerve to push out her chair and get up.

'If your stupid investigator had done a better job he would know I never *worked* for the Kulikovs. I went to school with Anais. We were best friends. I would have done anything for her. And I won't let you wreck her little boy's life. I'm one hundred per cent sure if Anais had known the future she would have named *me* Kostya's guardian. You're Leo's work. *Leo* made the mistake. Kostya shouldn't have to pay for it.'

She took a deep sustaining breath, taking some satisfaction that he looked pale and tense, but also horribly aware she had said some cruel things. But he had too. He had said she wanted to go to bed with him for *money*. He had *hurt* her.

'You lucked out, Alexei. I don't want anything from you. I thought I wanted to make love with you, but now I've never wanted anything less.'

Swaying a bit on her heels, she didn't look at him. She just walked away. He didn't try to stop her. Lust didn't override loyalty. Family came first. And Maisy, however inviting, was just a woman. Women were everywhere, he thought cynically.

'That dress,' he said coolly after her. 'Nice for a nanny. Leo must have paid you well. I expect you're *very* expensive to keep, Maisy.'

'No one has ever kept me,' she defended herself over her bare shoulder.

'I bet.' It was a crass thing to say, and Alexei instantly regretted it.

His throwaway line hit Maisy square in the solar plexus. He made her feel like a whore in her pretty dress and her make-up. All the *effort* she'd gone to… She spun around, determined not to let him have the last word, only to find he was already on his feet and coming towards her, his expression contrite, as if he'd realised he'd gone too far. But she'd moved too quickly, and her spindly heels wouldn't support the shift in her weight, and she went sprawling, jarring her shoulder as she tried to break her fall with one arm. Pain speared up her arm, making her cry out, and then she was lying on the ground, holding her arm and sucking back tears.

Alexei was on his knees beside her instantly, his arms coming around her. But as he touched her shoulder she cried out again.

'Let me help you,' he said gently, his anger no longer evident.

Maisy was too shaken up to protest, but as he lifted her she was thrown into immediate physical intimacy with him and it robbed her of breath. She could feel his biceps hard beneath her back, his big hand fastened around her thigh. He had to do these things to carry her, she reasoned wildly, but after the terrible things he had said to her the shivery reaction running through her body felt shameful. She averted her face from him, determined to block him out. If he saw how much he disturbed her it would just be more fuel for his accusations.

He carried her across the roof to the access door and down the stairs, as if she weighed nothing. Pain was pulsing through her shoulder, but the sheer awfulness of how cruelly his taunts had gone home overwhelmed it. He thought she was a liar, a party girl who spread her legs for anybody with enough cash, and he didn't want her looking after Kostya.

She wanted to cry, but she couldn't show that weakness.

She had just made the biggest fool of herself in the history of her life, and now a man who couldn't stand her—moreover a man who was an utter pig of an unreconstructed idiot, who couldn't see simple truths if they hit him in the face—was carrying her into...

His bedroom. Maisy's heartbeat sped up despite the pain.

And wasn't this what you were hoping for at the beginning of the night, Maisy Edmonds? a little voice niggled at her.

His bed was large and plain and masculine, with expensive dark blue linen. Fresh sheets, she registered. Had he been planning to seduce her here? Everything he had said to her came home, and she knew with every inch of her body she didn't want to be in here. It was too humiliating.

She began to struggle. 'Put me down. Put me down *now*!'

He was forced to release her and she slid to her feet, holding her arm folded over her chest. It was throbbing, but she had no intention of playing victim.

Alexei didn't say a word. He just made a phone call whilst she stood there, not sure what to do. He finished the call. 'A doctor's coming up to the house,' he said heavily. 'Where is the pain coming from?'

'I don't know. I think I jarred it,' she answered, swallowing hard. 'I'll go and wait in my room, if you don't mind.'

'Maisy, you had a nasty fall. Lie down here and let yourself to be checked out, okay?'

It sounded so reasonable, and the pain was pumping through

her body. But she kept seeing the look on his face when she'd told him the truth about the Kulikovs. It shouldn't matter so much, but it did.

In the end the pain won out and she sat down awkwardly on his bed. Alexei did something surprising. He dropped to one knee and reached for her foot, sliding off one shoe and then the other. There was something about seeing him silent on his knees in front of her that made her say, 'It's not your fault I fell. I did that to myself.'

'How's your arm?' he asked quietly, not making a move.

'I think it's going numb,' she said in a small voice.

'You landed at a bad angle.' He lifted his hand, hesitated, and then gently smoothed the tangle of curls that had been disturbed and now fell over one side of her face. Maisy swallowed. 'I'd give you some painkillers, but I think we should wait until the doctor has a look.'

'Okay.' The truth was she didn't want to be alone—not when her body felt as if it was in shock. And it wasn't only the fall. The implications of everything he had thrown at her were beginning to sink in.

The doctor was an urbane older man who clearly knew Alexei. He was scrupulously polite to Maisy as he examined her shoulder and prescribed painkillers, which he handed over to Alexei with instructions. Nothing was broken. Sleep and time would heal her.

'I'm a fraud,' she said tiredly. 'Nothing broken after all.'

Alexei sat down beside her on the bed. 'Take these, Maisy,' he said, and pressed two white pills against her lips.

More physical proximity she couldn't handle. Maisy drew them in with her tongue, brushing against his fingers, blushing. He'd think she was coming on to him.

He poured a little water into her mouth and she swallowed them down. His thumb lingered on her bottom lip and Maisy gazed back at him, startled, feeling heavy and tired and numb. She shifted awkwardly as the boning in her bodice dug hard.

'I need to get my dress off,' she said uncomfortably. 'I can't sleep in it.'

'Right.' He reached behind her, his fingers starting on the dozen tiny fabric buttons. His touch whispered down her back and Maisy shut her eyes, wishing everything was different. 'That's the problem with couture,' he said in a deep voice. 'No zips.'

'Anais gave it to me. I didn't know it was couture,' answered Maisy dully. 'I never looked.'

She caught her bodice with her good arm as the dress sprung free. She sat there, huddled in it, looking anxiously over her shoulder at him.

'If you turn your back I can stand up and drop it and then get into bed,' she explained awkwardly. She waited miserably for him to make some crack about it being a lousy attempt to seduce him.

Instead he said quietly, 'Of course.'

He was so formal she could only stare at him as he stood up and turned his back.

Maisy got off the bed and dropped the frock. Self-consciously she stepped out of the dress and kicked it away, shifting back onto the bed, pulling the cover up to her neck.

'Thank you,' she said awkwardly.

The pillow felt blissful beneath her head. She could feel the drugs beginning to take effect. Alexei scooped up her beautiful dress.

'I'll leave you now,' he said, in that oddly formal way. 'If you need anything just call out. I'm in the room across the hall.'

Maisy closed her eyes, damming up the tears that were brimming. She sensed the moment the lights went out.

'This wasn't how I envisaged the end of our evening,' she heard him say in a low voice from across the room.

I know, she thought miserably.

CHAPTER FIVE

MAISY opened her eyes in the vast bed to a low-grade headache and a great deal of self-recrimination as the memory of last night swamped her. She thrust her head under the pillow.

Of *his* bed.

She bolted upright, panic setting in as she realised she didn't have a shred of clothing to wear. She was trapped in his bed in her lacy knickers. After everything he had said to her last night the last thing she wanted was to be accused of angling for sex. Because that was what he'd come out and accused her of—being some sort of bimbo on the make, cavorting in couture. Ridiculous as that was.

Oh, Lord, where was her dress? The last she'd seen of it he had been carrying it away with him. Surely there were some clothes in this room?

Wrapping her arms across her bare breasts, she ran to some double doors. They opened onto a walk-in wardrobe and she spotted his shirts immediately, grabbing the nearest one and sliding her injured arm carefully into one sleeve, then the other. She had trouble with the left side buttonholes, but eventually got it done up decently enough. The shirt tails dangled almost to her knees. She went into the bathroom and washed the raccoon make-up off her face, running a hand through her unruly hair. She had to admit she didn't look that bad, all things considered, and the pain in her shoulder was now just a dull ache that should fade in a day or two.

All that had really got hurt last night was her pride.

Other thoughts intruded now. She remembered how gentle he had been with her when he'd realised she was hurt, how he had looked after her and how good that had felt. She had made the mistake of opening up to him a little, but he didn't want to hear it. She needed to remember that. Leo's death was still too raw for him. Only the knowledge that Alexei's feelings for his friend ran that deep gave her any comfort this morning, and that was in regards to Kostya.

As for what he had said in regards to *them*, she probably should thank him. At least now she wouldn't make an idiot of herself over him. He wasn't going to kiss her again. He might have—he might have done a great many things. Until she opened her big mouth and brought up Leo and Anais. Now he thought she was a liar, and apparently angling to be a kept woman. If it wasn't so offensive she would be laughing about it. Damn him, he owed her an apology.

Maisy glared at her reflection. She was going to get one.

Alexei felt like twenty kinds of bastard this morning as he pulled on a pair of jeans and nothing else.

He'd been so focussed on sexual conquest last night he'd barely appreciated Maisy's company, but a long night with only his thoughts had replayed her laughter and her absurd commentary about his lifestyle and made him sorry he hadn't tried to open her up a little more. But he'd closed all that down, slinging insults at her as she just sat there, completely defenceless. He had pretty much called her a whore, with nothing to support that accusation.

In fact he was starting to suspect Maisy's sexuality was as artless as the rest of her. She wasn't selling something, and—surprise, surprise—he didn't want to buy her. He didn't know exactly what it was he wanted from her, but he knew a beautiful girl in a stunning dress shouldn't be pushed so far, end up so distressed, she lost her balance trying to escape his cruel taunts. She was lying in his bed in pain because he couldn't deal with his goddamned issues.

This wasn't him. He didn't lose control like that. Especially with a woman. Especially not this woman. Maisy's uncomplicated sweetness was what he needed right now, so why was he pushing her away?

Barefoot and bare-chested, he crossed the hall. He lifted his hand to knock as his door swept open. She was standing there in one of his shirts, face scrubbed, amazingly beautiful.

'I want to know why you have such a low opinion of me,' she said bluntly.

The shock of seeing her like this, clearly strong and ready to take him on again, put him off balance. The combination of bare legs and *his* shirt made it difficult for him to think straight. Yet he was compelled to mutter, 'I don't have a low opinion of you.'

She stared back at him as if butter wouldn't melt in her mouth, although her eyes were all over his bare skin. 'Then maybe you could be a little nicer to me.'

Nice? She wanted him to be nice?

'How's your shoulder?'

'A little touchy, but I don't want to talk about my shoulder.'

'Neither do I, but it's good to know.' And in one movement he heaved her up over his shoulder and with his foot kicked shut the door behind them.

Oh, my.

'What are you doing?' she managed, although it would have been fairly clear to Blind Freddy what was going on. He was going to finish what he'd started in London right now, here, on this bed that was suddenly under her, and she was looking up into his laser-blue eyes and every one of her fantasies was pulsating to life.

'Yes or no, Maisy. Your decision.'

Yes, screamed her body, shifting from zero to a hundred in under two seconds. *But you hardly know him. Nice girls don't do this. Anais made Leo wait three months...*

Then he ran his thumbs gently over the inside of her wrists, lifting one of her hands to press his mouth where his thumb had been. Maisy made a soft little sound and he lifted her arms up over her head so that her breasts lifted and her body stretched out for him. He lowered himself down over her, hovering, his weight on his forearms, overwhelming her with the sheer size and strength of his body.

She broke the connection of their gaze to sweep a comprehensive look down his body, poised above hers. The faint press of his ribs, the slabs of muscle across his chest and shoulders and back, bunched as he bore the weight of his own body. It all combined to make her feel small and soft and feminine, and she wanted to touch him so badly her palms were burning.

'What do you want, Maisy?'

His scintillating blue eyes were so deep in hers Maisy found it hard to gather her words. Her heartbeat was so loud she was being deafened by it.

'I want everything,' she confided, her breath catching in her throat. 'I want you.'

Something flared in his eyes that caused a tug deep in her pelvis, and she half rose up off the mattress to meet him as he lowered his head to kiss her, long and slow and with a deep satisfaction. As if they had all the time in the world. But he kept her arms pinned so that she felt vulnerable to him in this position, her breasts rubbing slightly against his chest, her nipples sharpened with nerve endings and pressing against him shamelessly.

It felt incredibly good, yet when she tried to shift her arms his hands slid over hers and made it impossible for her to move. The more she strained against him the deeper he kissed her, her breasts sliding and pushing against him. Then he released her.

Stunned, Maisy lay alone on the bed as he leapt up. For a moment she didn't know what was going on, until full morning sunshine rushed into the room. Alexei had activated the blinds on the windows, letting in some light on the subject. Maisy blinked furiously as it hit her in the face. She brought her arms down, pressing on her good elbow as she struggled to sit up, confused and wondering exactly what she was getting herself into.

Alexei stepped in front of her so that she was forced to remain seated, gazing up at him. For one simmering moment he just stood there, looking down at her, those jeans sitting tantalisingly low on his lean hips. His abdomen was so ripped she longed to trace her fingers along the fine delineations of muscle. He was that close. A light smattering of dark chest hair covered him before arrowing down and disappearing into the V of his taut pelvic cradle. Maisy followed it with her eyes, her mouth running dry as she registered the distinct bulge. He surely didn't want that? Now? Did he? Was she supposed to start confessing everything she didn't know about the male body?

'Stop thinking, Maisy,' he instructed her, his voice warm with humour. 'Shift over, *dushka*.'

Feeling off-centre and decidedly gauche, Maisy scooted over into the centre of the bed, wondering if she should say something—if she was supposed to be doing something a more sophisticated woman would just know in her bones how to do. But he was coming down over her, blocking out the sun, and suddenly all she could see and feel and inhale was him.

He brushed his lips over her mouth, and when she instinctively responded he moved away to drop butterfly kisses along her jawline. Maisy began to sense he was playing a game with her, one of advance and retreat, as if tightening his hold on her each time. She didn't want London, she didn't want out-of-control, but nor did she want to play a part in any sort of game. She wanted simple, she thought nervously as her body responded despite her jangling thoughts. She wanted honest. She just wanted *him*.

Maybe she should tell him.

Then his breath was hot in her ear and he began to promise her things…wicked things, sexual things…and then he shifted slightly, and she was pinned under the heft of his body, and she felt every inch of what he wanted to do with her.

Oh, my.

Maisy lost her ability to think, the wicked images he had put in her head heating her blood. She wrapped her arms around his neck to anchor him to her and made her own soft, satisfied sound under the impact of his mouth on hers. She winced as her shoulder gave a sharp tug and he instantly rolled onto his back, his arm around her waist, to pull her over on top of him.

For an instant she felt a wave of disappointment. Was he going to pull away from her again?

Instead he framed her face with his big hands. 'Better for your shoulder,' he muttered against her mouth, lifting to kiss her again, and a rush of real warmth ran through Maisy because he was looking after her.

Being on top also allowed her to set the pace. She fused her mouth to his, tasting the salt and spice and goodness of him, her hands meshing in his hair as she swept her tongue into his mouth. She had absolutely no idea what she was doing. She knew the mechanics, what went where, but her single dismal experience had left her with very little understanding of what he was going to like. She hoped if she pleased herself it would please him too.

His hands were on her back, searching for the ends of his shirt and rucking it up. He spread his fingers over her cool bare skin, sweeping his hands down over her hips until he had the little scrap of lace clinging to her bottom beneath his fingers. He squeezed the lush weight of her buttocks and her knees dropped instinctively to either side of his hips. The impressive erection contained in his jeans was nestled in exactly the right spot for her, and he groaned as Maisy gave an experimental wriggle, then settled over him. He obliged, using his hands on her hips to work her rhythmically against him.

Maisy began to pant, making little gasping noises, and Alexei thought the sound alone was going to undo him. It was incredible. He felt like a teenage boy all over again, barely able to keep a leash on the urges rushing through his body. It was all Maisy—the feel and smell and look of her, and the way she used his body to satisfy herself. Something had tipped in her favour early on in this encounter and he had lost the upper hand. If he'd ever had it. He began to growl her name and her thighs clenched around him.

That deep note in his voice always pulled on her inner muscles, and combined with the friction of him under her it lit the match and Maisy moaned, body taut, as her core dissolved into liquid sunshine. Unable to believe what had happened, she pressed her mouth into the base of his throat, face blood-red, and trembled on top of him with tiny aftershocks. Oh, God— she had used him as a sex toy.

Alexei was sitting her up, moving her on past the moment, so that she was virtually straddling his lap. His bigger body made her feel small and delicate in his arms, vulnerable to him in this position. Stripped to the waist, the spread of his chest was available to her hands and she began touching him, marvelling at the strength beneath the hot skin, meshing her fingers in his light chest hair, nuzzling him with her nose and mouth, running her tongue over his flat nipples until he hissed. The sound surged through Maisy's body, giving her a much needed boost in confidence.

His hands were actually shaking as he got busy at the buttons of his shirt.

'Okay, Maisy?' His eyes sought hers again as his fingers kept on moving down the shirt.

She swayed against him and their mouths met, mingled. Maisy got a little lost in the kissing until his lips left hers, and then she looked down and saw the deep valley between her breasts had come into view. Alexei's stunning hot gaze did not shift from that moment on as he peeled the shirt open.

Alexei said something under his breath and then his big hands were splaying over them, catching up her nipples. He bent his head to take one into his mouth. His bristle-roughened chin abraded her sensitive skin as he suckled and fondled and nuzzled her, ignoring her efforts to touch him in kind until she was unbearably anxious to feel him inside her. She had not imagined in her wildest dreams she would feel this driven. It wasn't in her nature, wasn't in *her*—until now.

She put her hands on his waistband but his hands were already there, pushing her away.

'Not yet, *dushka*,' he rasped, lying her back flat on the bed and kissing down her belly to the scrap of white lace she was wearing.

She could feel her whole face suffusing in a hot blush of reaction. He edged off her knickers so slowly it felt like for ever. She was almost relieved when they were off. Then he went sliding to his knees on the floor, dragging her legs after him, so for a moment her knees hooked over his shoulders.

Maisy stopped breathing. It was an unbearably intimate position—especially when she looked down—and she wriggled, a wave of embarrassment passing over her. Then she felt him begin to blow air over the moist core of her, and she bit the fleshy part of her hand to keep from crying out.

Dan hadn't done this. Dan hadn't been anywhere near down there with his mouth. She'd read about it, but the reality was liquefying.

When he parted her and she felt his fingers slide into her she keened, and when his tongue ran over her clitoris her hips began to undulate on the bed. She didn't care how loud she was being. It didn't take long until her inner walls were tugging on his fingers as he slid them out of her, and his tongue dragged over the sweet centre of her one last time before he stood up, unhooking his jeans with suddenly clumsy fingers.

Maisy lay there watching him, her cheeks red, her eyes bright, her body unbelievably lush in his eyes. From her softly rounded arms to her breasts, the curve of her little waist to stunningly flared hips, the solidity of her female thighs and the taper of her calves down to her pretty feet. She was a pink-and-white study in eroticism, with the golden fire of her tumbled curls and the red-gold at the apex of her thighs a touch of genius.

An artist would give a great deal to paint her like this; a

man would give his soul just to look upon her. That he was getting it all sent Alexei into overdrive. He didn't want to be out of control with her, but he could already feel himself slipping and sliding towards mindless pleasure. The things he could do to her—the places he could take her if she would let him. And he knew she would let him. And every primitive male instinct in his body charged to the fore.

She sat up slowly, as if knowing not to rush her movements, and replaced his clumsy hands with her own, gently popping every last button.

He had a look of incredible concentration on his face, and as his jeans hit the floor Maisy's mouth made a perfect circle of wonder. *This* was not what she was used to. She ran a fingertip along the heavy veined shaft, wondering how on earth they were going to fit. He put his hand over hers and drew her fingers over him, around him, up and down, giving her voiceless instruction on how much pressure he needed, the speed.

Just watching him made her tremble. The force of him, the weight of his desire was almost too much. Maisy knew she had just hit the deep end and could no longer feel the bottom. He unwrapped her hand but kept hold of it, anchoring her back on the bed, coming over her. He kissed her with the full force of his mouth, his hands sliding down under her lush behind to lift her and position her.

'I want you under me the first time,' he muttered into her mouth, as if she needed telling.

Maisy felt him brush at her entrance, his blunt tip penetrating her. She reached up to stroke his face, wanting him to be looking at her, seeking a connection with him. He went a little further and then swore under his breath, pulled out of her, drew back, stood up.

'Don't move,' he instructed.

Alexei was tearing open a foil packet, and she watched as he dealt with the necessities, sheathing himself at speed, so that she was reminded he had done this far too many times. *Whilst I've only done it once*, she thought, her heart pounding.

He hadn't taken his eyes off her, and as he positioned himself over her again he paused to lean in and kiss her again—a kiss that told her he knew who she was.

He sank slowly into her, moving with stealth, as if relishing the surprisingly tight clasp of her. Maisy began to lift her hips to coax him, bring him into her. Bring him home. Her eyes flared wide as he fully seated himself. His shoulders were braced above her, the muscles heavy across his shoulders and chest. He looked down at her with the intent expression of a man who knew absolutely what he was doing. He framed her face with one hand.

'Okay, Maisy?' His voice was strained, his whole body tensed above her.

It was the second time he had asked her that, and she liked it. She liked it so much she thought her chest might explode with feeling. It showed he cared about her. In answer she wrapped her good arm around his strong neck and brought his mouth down to hers.

Her body had taken over now, and that tiny doubt planted in that grimy room in Earls Court was exploded in the time it took Alexei to fully penetrate her. *This* was her man, the right man. He knew exactly what to do, and her body responded in kind. He drove her higher and higher, until she was hanging over the edge of a cliff with her fingertips. When she fell he came with her, and she clung tight to him as he thrust again and again, her brain on hiatus as she gave herself over to the sheer joy of being a part of him.

When he sank forward, his head pressed to the curve of her neck, she held him as tightly as he would let her for as long as he would let her, and when he pulled out of her and rolled onto his back he rewarded her by taking her with him.

'I don't usually do this.'

Alexei couldn't think. But that wasn't surprising, given he was still coming down the other side of an incredible orgasm. He knew his brain would flick the functioning switch in a

minute, but right now all he could do was say her name—
Maisy—and run his hand happily down the full round flank
of her bottom and thigh. Her head lay on his chest—all those
long ringlets cascading over them—her smooth thigh rested
on his hair-roughened front quad muscle, and he could feel
the hot wet centre of her pressed against him. There were so
many things he wanted to do with her, and just anticipating
the weeks to come made his blood hum.

But she was saying something. She was sitting up, and managed to pull the sheet around her as he watched her. 'What
don't you usually do?' He didn't want to move, but he wished
she would drape herself back across him.

'This. Have casual sex.'

The words sounded a bit harsh. He was thinking *incredible*
sex. Surely he'd covered all the bases? She'd definitely come
apart in his arms. She should be purring like a kitten, but instead she was sitting there, huddling in a sheet, talking about
casual sex.

Then the other shoe dropped. Of course. She wanted to
hear that he respected her, that they would be repeating this
regularly—for a while—and then she'd drop the sheet and
crawl back into his space.

He could do all that. He would, once his brain clicked into
gear. But some other part of him said, with a sincerity he didn't
recognise, 'Nothing about this is casual, Maisy.'

She had the softest eyes in the world, he thought, arrested
for a moment by the expression on Maisy's face. And somehow he had said exactly the right thing, because some of the
tension had run out of her and she looked both shy and hopeful.

How in the hell was she shy after what they'd just done?
What they were going to do? With her face flushed, her round
hazel eyes dilated, she looked like a woman who had enjoyed
very satisfactory sex. She also looked a little embarrassed.

It was sweet. He reached for her and she came to him, soft
and warm and accommodating. Exactly what he wanted from

her. He laid his hand between her legs, easing them apart as his fingers found her sensitive part and slid in and out of the hot wet core of her. His eyes never left the expression on her face as he built her orgasm out of the remains of what had gone before.

CHAPTER SIX

'I HAD wild uninhibited sex in broad daylight. I had *lots* of wild, uninhibited sex in broad daylight,' Maisy confided to the pillow, as if this were a secret, and Alexei laughed. The sound was so reassuring Maisy subsided into the vibrations of his chest, wanting to stay curled against him for as long as possible. His large, tight-muscled frame took up more than half the bed, but she didn't mind.

Alexei ran a possessive hand over her hip, now covered by a single sheet. He had so thoroughly explored her body in the last two hours he couldn't imagine a freckle or dimple he wasn't familiar with, but she insisted on covering herself, revealing a modesty that oddly touched him.

He pulled her tighter into the shelter of his body.

He never did cuddling.

He performed, he took his pleasure, and then he showered and dressed and left.

Maisy curled against him, as if heat-seeking, her closing lashes soft on her round cheeks. He'd exhausted her, and the thought satisfied an entirely primitive, unreconstructed part of himself.

The more sophisticated part of him was planning ahead. How to fit her into his schedule; how to set the parameters of their relationship...

She has no idea who I am or what I require of her, he thought, and it was an oddly charged feeling—one he didn't want to relinquish yet. He couldn't quite put his finger on it, but for a time he had felt a barrier come down. He'd felt free to just luxuriate in this closeness. Soon enough they would have to get out of bed and harsh reality would intrude. He didn't want clingy, didn't want emotions, didn't want a *relationship*. He wanted sex. In return he would give her anything she desired.

Foremost, he didn't want her to nurture any illusions about him.

Then why did it feel as if he was shutting her out and in the process shutting down a part of himself?

He bedded glamorous women for a reason. It had nothing to do with their allure. Hell, he doubted they were even his *type*. But they came with a pack drill. They knew what they were about, they knew what they wanted, and they knew what he was offering. There were limits to these liaisons. Tara had been a perfect example.

But just the thought of her this morning ran a chill through him, and he tightened his arms around Maisy. Tara was a reminder of why Maisy had snuck in under his radar. This uncomplicated sweetness was what he wanted—probably needed. Maisy had come to him with nothing but her wonderful, warm, accommodating body.

Peace was what he was feeling, and in answer to it he rolled her onto her back and settled himself across her, cradling his head on her belly.

It would be good for them both. She clearly hadn't had much of a life, from what she'd told him with her mum and the gig with Anais's baby. He could offer her luxury, travel and a speed dial for her sexual repertoire. He in turn would get this much joy and sweetness in his bed.

And he would not let himself be weak and mistake it for anything else.

He shoved that thought aside and luxuriated in the feeling of her. After everything that had gone before it was like being reborn. He needed six months of Maisy. In fact if he was a doctor he'd recommend it.

She smelled so good—warm female skin, the faint traces of the tangerine soap she used, and sex. She hadn't rushed off to wash herself and it was nice, just lying here with her, feeling the rise and fall of her breathing under his head, knowing she wasn't going anywhere.

She sat up, dislodging his head. 'Kostya,' she said.

Realising a response was required from him, Alexei gazed up at her, a smile of disbelief on his slumberous face. 'Relax, Maria will get him up.'

'I always get him up,' Maisy protested, swinging her legs off the bed, trying to drag the sheet with her.

Alexei had no intention of moving. 'Come back to bed, *dushka*. Maria can look after him today.'

Even as he said it Alexei registered Maisy's disapproval.

She made a dash for his shirt and thrust her arms frantically into the sleeves, covering herself as quickly as she could. She didn't say anything, and the longer that went on the more annoyed Alexei was feeling. The baby was *fine*. *He* needed a bit of attention. Where in the hell was she going?

'Maisy!' He didn't like the bark in his voice, and Maisy clearly didn't either. She swung around, hair flying, frowning at him as if he had offended her. 'Please come back to bed,' he said with studied patience.

Maisy shook her head. 'I can't,' she said.

'Fine.' He bounded off the bed and headed for the bathroom. He was going to shower and start the day. Maisy needed to know who was in charge.

'Where are you going?' she said.

'The entertainment is over. I need a shower and a shave,' he shot back at her.

Maisy paled. Her anxiety to get downstairs to the nursery dulled as the impact of that word pinned her to the spot.

Entertainment.

She stood staring at the open bathroom door. She felt as if he'd slapped her. He couldn't mean it. She wanted to run after him and tackle him, demand he take it back, but there wasn't time.

Kostya.

She kept moving, her heart pounding as she skittered along the hallway, praying no one appeared around the corner to find her naked except for a man's shirt. Alexei's shirt. Everyone would know what they had been doing, if they didn't already. It wouldn't matter so much if it was the beginning of some sort of a relationship; it mattered a great deal to her if he thought of her as providing 'entertainment'.

Her heartbeat began to slam inside her chest, heavy and dull, as reality laid a cold hand on her shoulder. All the drama of last night came rushing back. He'd said some pretty hurtful things and he hadn't taken one of them back. As if sex cancelled it all out. Although for him it probably did. He seemed very pleased with himself. And why wouldn't he be? One meal and she was on her back. What sort of girl jumped into bed with a man so quickly?

Emotions were roiling through her and she could barely keep a lid on them. Oh, God. It was all too clear. She had made a huge leap of faith, and he had had a one-night stand.

She had to walk through the nursery to get to her room. The realisation brought her to a halt. She couldn't walk in like this—not if Kostya wasn't alone.

Trying not to think about the humiliation to come, she retraced her steps. She could hear the sound of running water. She took a deep breath and walked into the luxurious bathroom. Alexei was standing under a waterfall of water, head down, shoulders hunched. His beautiful long lean body took her breath away, still. Knowing he was an absolute bastard didn't change that.

He looked up as he sensed her presence, his lips parting. He cut off the water. 'Changed your mind, *dushka*?'

There was something about that endearment, that *casual* endearment, that twisted the knife. Maisy blocked the truckload of pain she could feel coming and said, 'I need my dress. Where did you put my dress?'

'A little cold in the shirt, Maisy?' He grabbed a towel and began drying his hair, completely unselfconscious about his nudity.

Maisy focussed her eyes on a spot across the room and repeated, 'I need my dress.'

'I heard you.' He casually wrapped the towel around his lean hips and knotted it. 'It's safe to look, *dushka*. Although I've got no idea what's spooked you, Maisy. It's not as if you haven't been introduced.'

She wanted to hit him.

That did it.

Maisy stepped up to him and for a moment she fancied he actually looked expectant—as if she was going to launch herself into his arms after everything he had said and done.

Bastard. She slapped him as hard as she could across his face. His head jarred slightly to the right and then slowly came around again to stare down at her. Maisy took a backward step.

He brought a hand slowly up to his jaw and rubbed. 'Feel better?'

'No.'

'I'll get your dress.'

It was all over. She could still feel where he had been inside her and yet it was over, Maisy registered. She couldn't believe she had hit him. He was cold, arrogant, self-centered, and she was…on the premises and…happy to oblige.

That was how it was, wasn't it?

Yet as the seconds turned into minutes she began to lose her ground. Maria would be with Kostya, as she was every morning. The realisation had stolen up on her even before she'd walked in here, and now it bloomed with full force. She had overreacted. She had been lying in that bed, suddenly feeling alone and self-conscious, terrified of what was to come, what this sudden new intimacy meant, and she had run away rather than face it. Somehow she had convinced herself that if the sex stopped he wouldn't want her in the bed, and she'd felt too raw to face that so she had jumped out. He might be angry with her now, but that didn't mean everything was over before it began.

Alexei had reacted appallingly, but at least he was fetching her dress. Dan hadn't even given her the taxi fare home.

A soft gust of bittersweet amusement at her overreaction made her drop her head. She was hopeless at all this men stuff, but she would get better.

His arms came around her from behind and she was drawn up into a bear hug that turned her insides to mush. 'I'm sorry,' he muttered against her ear.

Maisy turned and burrowed deep into him and hung on. Relief made her limp.

Alexei rested his chin on the top of her warm head and released a deep sigh. 'Go and see Kostya.'

It was, she recognised, a magnanimous gesture. He wasn't used to making room for other people in his life, yet here he was making space for Kostya, putting his needs first. Maybe accommodating *her* a little.

I'm being considerate, thought Alexei, enjoying the results of a clinging Maisy. *I'm attuned to her feelings*. Wasn't that the current jargon? But something in him regretted having hurt her.

Maisy reacted predictably for once, turning up her face to be kissed and reassured. He knew the drill. But there was no kiss. That little crease was back between her brows.

'What am I going to tell Maria if she asks where I've been?'

Maria? Who cared about the housekeeper? 'My sex life is not Maria's business.'

The little crease deepened. 'Not you—me.'

'Maisy, I chased you down to Ravello yesterday. I had dinner with you on the rooftop. Everybody knows.'

She blushed.

She blushed—after two hours of lying naked under him and over him.

But there were certain things she didn't do, he registered,

and when he led her in some directions she did not come with him. It hadn't mattered—he'd been so caught up in the sheer impact of being with her.

It was unlikely, but he had to ask.

'Maisy, were you a virgin?'

'I can't believe you asked me that.' She tried to wriggle out of his arms, but suddenly Alexei could think of no better way to spend the next five minutes than drilling Maisy for some personal information.

Women usually spilled their guts on the first encounter— gave him well-edited potted histories of their empty lives until he and his billions walked into their world. One Hollywood actress had tried to persuade him she had never enjoyed sex until him. He might have been flattered had he not seen her by the pool of his home in Florida intimately entwined with another woman.

He watched Maisy squirm, her round cheeks hot and pink, her red-gold curls a tangled out-of-control mass. She was using it to hide her face from him. He knew he could never let her know about *his* former life. She would be horrified. Little hot-to-trot Maisy had a great deal of girl-next-door in her.

He'd known it yesterday afternoon, when he'd climbed back into the Ferrari and seen her mortification. She wasn't a gold-digger. She was just a little out of her depth. When he'd lowered the levels she had risen to meet him. He'd been rewarded with the most incredible sex he had ever had.

Be nice to me. Even the sound of her voice stoked him. She loaded the simplest words with carnal meaning. Yet here she was blushing, embarrassed.

He'd read her wrong. Again. Not only was she a good girl, she was a romantic.

'How many men, Maisy?'

He knew he should have framed that question more sensitively, but he didn't *do* sensitive.

'How many women, Alexei?' She jerked up her face, embarrassed, but with that edge he was beginning to look forward to.

'Too many.' His answer surprised even himself.

She made a wry face, but he saw a flash of hurt in her eyes.

She must never know. It would tear a big hole in that romantic little soul of hers.

Stunned, Alexei wondered where that thought had come from. Pushing it aside, he gave her chin a gentle pinch.

'How many, Maisy?' he pressed.

'Just one. Once.'

She looked almost defiant as she said it, as if daring him to comment. Alexei, rocked by that little announcement, did his best to disguise it. He hadn't thought for one moment she was a virgin, but now he knew she might as well be.

'Could you tell?' she framed awkwardly as his silence stretched on.

He pushed the hair out of her eyes. 'I think I'm very lucky,' he said genuinely.

It was clearly the right thing to say.

Maisy sprang up and squeezed him around the neck. She was happy. He had made Maisy happy for the first time since they'd climbed out of bed and everything had gone pear-shaped. There was a lesson there. Keep her horizontal as often as possible.

But there was Kostya to consider.

'Kostya,' she said, right on schedule.

'I'll go.' He didn't know why he volunteered, but he was beginning to understand any chance of uninterrupted play with Maisy could only be engineered if he loosened her grip on Kostya.

Besides, it was time to build a relationship with the boy.

Maisy was fastening herself back into her white gown when there was a knock on the door. She froze.

'Miss Edmonds?'

She recognised the voice and went to open the door. It was one of the girls from the kitchen. She merely held out an armful of supplies: some fresh clothes and her bag of toiletries.

Maisy accepted them wordlessly, then remembered her manners and thanked the girl. Jeans and a T-shirt and plain cotton underwear. Alexei had not chosen these for her. She knew him now. She also knew he was not going to be discreet about any of this.

Well, Maisy, in for a penny, in for a pound.

She emptied the toiletries bag and found bubble bath. A bath. She was going to have a bath.

She filled Alexei's big tub, carefully hung up her dress, and submerged herself in warm sudsy water. Her spirit felt light. For the first time in a long time she felt young and desirable, and for the moment free of any responsibility except for herself. She stretched out her legs and draped her arms along the sides of the tub. Her body ached in an unfamiliar but entirely satisfying way.

Alexei had behaved as if he couldn't keep his hands off her and she had gloried in his obvious enjoyment of her body. He had been so tender with her, putting a lie to that 'entertainment' crack. Yet she couldn't ignore it. He had made it for a reason.

She sensed that, as much as he wanted her, his instinct was to push her away. Strange as the thought was, it was as if he had a wall around him. She'd felt it back at Lantern Square—how untouchable he seemed. Something had changed in the park yesterday. She'd seen the real man behind that wall when he'd hunkered down to Kostya's level to reassure him. That same sweetness had been in the way he had removed her shoes last night. In these moments he had been reachable, human, vulnerable.

But she sensed these glimpses were involuntary. He didn't want the closeness she sought. Even as he had kept her snug in his arms, she had instinctively known this was as much as he was offering.

She needed to be very careful. She needed to guard her heart.

Kostya was pleased to see Maisy. He got up and toddled across the terrace to throw up his arms for his morning cuddle.

Alexei noted approvingly that a cuddle was all he required and then he was struggling to be put down. He ran back to his pedal car. Observing the child this morning, he had been aware of what Maisy had said to him last night about Leo's absence and Anais's inability to cope. But Kostya appeared to be a well-adjusted little boy—no signs of clinginess or insecurity. Her claims just didn't add up. A huge part of him was relieved, but it worried him that she had lied. It didn't align with the girl he was beginning to know.

Alexei remained where he was, with a pile of newspapers from around the world, his smart phone and a strong espresso. It was a morning like any other when he wasn't working—except for Maisy. She had pulled up her hair into a ponytail and wore jeans and a V-necked T-shirt. He didn't want clingy—he didn't *do* clingy—but Maisy had taken it *way* in the opposite direction. Clearly they were pretending not to know one another. Interesting. He decided not to react to her, waiting for her to come to him.

Sipping his espresso, he idly thumbed through his schedule, lining up his phone appointments for the day.

Maisy poured herself a glass of orange juice from the buffet and approached the table uneasily, waiting for Alexei to look up, to speak, with half of her attention attuned to Maria—who must *know*. He'd turned up yesterday and this morning she was bouncing out of his bed. It was one thing to be a sexually independent woman. It was another thing to have an audience—a traditional Italian audience.

Before she sat down he half rose from his chair, his manners clearly so ingrained that even when he was ignoring her

he behaved like a gentleman. Maisy settled herself, still waiting to be spoken to. Nothing. She looked around. Maria was
clearing the buffet. Steadying her nerve, she watched Kostya
for a while. She was constantly aware of Alexei, typing into
his phone, stabbing with his thumb, and Maisy experienced his
uninterest like a well-placed kick to her fledgling sexual self-
confidence. It was exactly like the aftermath of her sleeping
with Dan. She had dressed in the cold whilst he had answered
emails, his back to her. Except this was worse—because as
she had buttoned herself up she had known she didn't care for
Dan and had no intention of repeating the experience.

This time she wanted to climb into Alexei's lap. Her insides
seemed to light up when she had his attention. Even now, as
he fiddled with that stupid device, she couldn't strip her eyes
off him, was wishing he would just look up and acknowledge
her. But she knew he wouldn't. It was the equivalent of dressing in the cold.

All of her insecurities came rushing back. Maybe he had
changed his mind. She might have been able to attract him
but she couldn't hold him. Her mind went helplessly back over
events, trying to find the flaws in their lovemaking. Had she
done something he didn't like? Had she not been responsive
enough? He had wanted her to take him in her mouth but she
hadn't felt confident enough. Maybe that was it?

She tried to sip her orange juice, but she was so tense it went
down the wrong way and she ended up in a coughing fit.

Alexei looked up as she set down the glass with a bump and
choked. Tears of reaction had sprung into her eyes, sparking the
deeply held pain she was nursing, and more brimmed and slid
down her cheeks. She swiped at her eyes, hoping he wouldn't
realise she was crying because of him. It would put the nail
in the coffin of her humiliation for him to see how deeply all
this was affecting her.

She pushed back her chair noisily, not looking at him.

'Where are you going?' He sounded genuinely surprised.

'I'm disturbing you,' she got out rapidly. 'I'll just go.'

'You haven't eaten any breakfast.'

He had noticed? She hadn't thought he'd even registered her presence.

'I'm not hungry.' She had to get away from him. She walked blindly down the terrace, blinking rapidly.

Then she heard Kostya's high little voice. 'Maisy!' And she had to go back for him.

However broken up she felt inside, she was all Kostya had. Funnily enough, he was all she had too. And as she hurried back the child met her halfway, arms extended to be lifted, cuddled, assured of her love. He was heavy, so she sank down onto the ground with him and rocked him in her arms, mustering a smile and reassuring chatter. She might be an abject failure with men, but she knew how to be a good mother to Kostya.

'You have to leave him with me today,' Alexei was saying. He was sauntering over, smart phone and papers abandoned, looking unaccountably edgy.

Maisy looked up, her eyes still wet so that her lashes had a starfish effect. Alexei tried to block the accompanying flash of emotion as he remembered how uninhibitedly she had given herself to him. Now she was acting as if she wanted to be anywhere but around him.

His first instinct was to reassure her, but it was clear she was carrying a bucketload of regrets. Well, tough. He wasn't going to apologise for enjoying her body so thoroughly. Maisy was built for a man's pleasure. Everything about her—from her wild glossy ringlets to the serious curve of her waist to the fulsome round of her bottom—sang to his libido. After too many women with borderline eating disorders, the curves and valleys of Maisy's small yet womanly body reduced him to drooling, uncontrolled lust. He fully intended to keep her and have her again and again.

He could deal with her regrets with jewellery. It always worked a treat with women's moods. Experience told him put a diamond pendant in the valley between those magnificent breasts of hers and she'd soon cheer up. He'd organise Carlo to have a selection sent down tomorrow.

Except deep down he knew jewellery would probably upset her.

But for now he had a small child to wrest from her arms. A thought which didn't make him feel particularly proud of himself. Especially with Maisy looking so incredibly vulnerable. It would be too easy to gather her up into his arms and soothe that edginess in her away. He'd played it cool this morning, aware of the staff observing them. Any other woman and it wouldn't have mattered, but Maisy had unaccountably befriended a good many of the people who worked for him. Those seven days he had left her alone here had backfired on him. Shy as she was around him at times, she clearly had no trouble drawing other people to her and holding them.

Everyone liked Maisy. Which was fine. Except it made *him* liking her slightly more awkward. He didn't know why, but he felt a distinct vibe of disapproval from Maria this morning. It was ridiculous. Maisy was over twenty-one, and she was a sexually active young woman—it made sense they'd ended up in bed together. He wouldn't be fulfilling his function as a fit and healthy twenty-nine-year-old male if he didn't drag her off to bed.

Yet that wasn't exactly how it had been. Maisy wasn't just some girl, and it hadn't felt like a function. It was the beginning of something—he just couldn't quite grasp what it was that was making him so uneasy. And this morning had been eminently worthwhile. In fact it had been a revelation.

Still, he had to separate this woman from this child, and do it with the least amount of trauma to either of them.

But Maisy was sitting there, being all that was motherly with Kostya, and it affected him. She was incredibly feminine— something he suspected was playing havoc with his usual defences in this kind of situation.

He would have had to be blind this morning not to see how relieved she was to have him confirm their encounter was not casual. And now she was everything soft and tender, cradling the child in her arms, looking exactly like the kind of woman a nice guy would want to protect and cherish and probably marry. Hell, she had 'wife material' written all over her. Absolutely off-limits to a guy like him. Yet he'd gone ahead and infiltrated her affections anyway.

It was about time he made sure she understood. He didn't want her to nurture any illusions about him. He was a bastard, and Maisy needed to understand that before she started confusing what he was offering her with happy families and swamping them both in unnecessary and dangerous emotion.

The thought assailed him that he wasn't exactly clear on what he was offering her, and for one tiny moment he allowed himself a glimpse of just what a relationship with Maisy might look like.

Which was probably why he didn't pull any of his next punches.

'Maisy, if you're worried about Maria stop it now.'

'That's easy for you to say,' she muttered.

'Maria is accustomed to female guests coming down to breakfast in a great deal less than you're wearing, *dushka*. I wouldn't let it bother you.'

He knew it was a brutal thing to say. Something flinched inside as he actually witnessed the moment she took his meaning. Her eyes flew to his, and then flashed away as she turned her face into Kostya's curls.

Alexei felt cold to his stomach. *Congratulations*, he thought, *you're a bigger bastard than you thought*.

With the rug pulled from under her, Maisy scrambled for a foothold in this strange new world. How on earth was she going to stay here with him and pretend to be okay with all this? A little voice reminded her he wasn't *trying* to insult her—he was just telling her how it was. It wasn't as if she'd imagined he lived like a monk, but for him to actually *tell* her she was one in a queue was probably the hardest thing she would ever have to hear from him. Until he said goodbye. Which, clearly, would be sooner rather than later.

But the truth wasn't what she wanted this morning. She wanted a show of affection and his hand in hers…and a little reassurance.

What she got was a man who had put in the time for sexual gymnastics first thing, but was keen to put it all behind him now the day had begun.

'So, will you be spending the day with Kostya?' Maisy was proud of how level she sounded—as if the waves of pain crashing over her were being deflected by a larger sense of self-preservation.

'Why don't you spend it with us?'

He actually sounded gentler, but Maisy couldn't bring herself to look at him. She started when he reached down to lift Kostya from her arms, and felt a twinge of regret when Kostya went so willingly. Maisy didn't know what to do now. She felt awkward sitting at his feet, with images of the intimacies they had shared shredding the atmosphere between them. She couldn't go back, she realised, panicked.

'I think I want to be alone for a while,' she said stolidly.

Stupid girl, stupid girl, stupid girl.

She clambered to her feet, feeling ungraceful and at a disadvantage, and walked as fast as she could across the terrace, not aware of where she was going, just conscious of wanting to put some distance between herself and the rocks on which she had shipwrecked herself.

CHAPTER SEVEN

ALEXEI watched her go. Why had he opened his big mouth? Why hurt her like this? It had barely begun and he was tearing shreds off her.

'Want Maisy,' wailed Kostya, clinging to his shirt front.

Alexei looked down at the infant's ominously reddening face. He was clearly reacting to all the tension. *I've stuffed this up*, Alexei thought flatly. 'I want Maisy too, *malenki chelovek*.'

She had reached the end of the terrace and he watched her hesitate, circle, looking for a way out. But this terrace led nowhere, and the glass doors were locked. For a moment he watched as she pushed at them, and then he saw her shoulders drop, saw her shake her head and lose heart.

That was enough.

He strode towards her, watched her face come up—her pale, lovely face—strained and tense. And *he* had put that tension there.

He hadn't meant to push her this far. He'd been trying for disengagement when all he was feeling was passionate connection. He hadn't meant to hurt her.

'Maisy, we need to talk. I'll hand Kostya over to Maria and then you're coming with me.' He reached for her hand, but she pulled away, eyes flashing.

'You're too late, Alexei,' she slung at him fiercely. 'I don't want to hear anything you have to say.'

Kostya released a huge cry and scrambled for Maisy. She

took him into her arms, flashing daggers over his curly head. 'Now look what you've done,' she breathed.

Alexei made a very male European gesture with one hand and pinned her with his incredible eyes. 'If you want to do it in front of the boy—fine. Here's the deal, Maisy.'

He spoke in a low, firm voice—the one she imagined he used in another life that didn't involve crying children and emotional women who refused to vanish after sex.

'This morning was incredible. I want to repeat it. Often. I want you in my life. Is that clear enough for you? Does that sort out the problem?'

Incredible. Repeat it. He wanted her in his life.

Maisy was sure he was wondering why she wasn't cheering. Instead his coolly delivered words struck a flint of anger inside her. 'I'm sure that works with all those other *female guests* of yours, but I require a little bit more finesse, Alexei, so I'm turning you down.'

'Fair enough.' He shrugged, and Maisy's face fell so fast it should have amused him. It didn't. 'I should have dragged you back to bed and manacled you to the bedpost,' he declared. 'But I don't bring women here. The handcuffs and paraphernalia are in my Rome apartment.'

Maisy huffed, trying to cover Kostya's ears. 'You're disgusting!'

'You weren't saying that around dawn, *dushka*. How in the hell are you still blushing?'

'I'm not used to stripping naked and bouncing around on a bed in broad daylight,' she snapped.

'Something that does incredible things for my ego,' he replied complacently.

Maisy huffed again.

He gave her an arrested look. 'You are adorable, Maisy.'

She suddenly couldn't wrest her eyes away from his. What was it he'd said about not bringing women here?

'We can't have this conversation in front of Kostya. Where's Maria?'

'*Now* she sees sense,' Alexei murmured, stroking the back of Kostya's head, managing to caress the back of Maisy's hand. She didn't pull away.

Kostya distracted with strawberry yoghurt in the kitchen, Maisy walked with Alexei down into the garden. As they lingered before a stone fountain amidst the greenery Alexei said, in a dark, suggestive voice, 'We could go back upstairs.'

'I won't answer that.' She turned her face away, but a little smile was tugging at her lips.

'We could do it here.'

Maisy gasped. 'I'm not making love to you in a garden. Anyone could see.'

He smiled slowly at her. 'You're right. I'm very possessive, Maisy, as you'll learn. I don't want any other man seeing you when you climax.'

'You're so confident I would?' she whispered, unsure they wouldn't be overheard. She suddenly imagined dozens of men hiding in the bushes.

'Would what? Wrap those lovely legs around my waist or climax?'

'Both,' she snapped.

'I can't force you, Maisy, but I can guarantee the climax.'

He was outrageous. Maisy loved it. She bit her lip. She didn't want to forgive him so soon, but her heart was racing and her skin was prickling and suddenly all she wanted was to wrap herself around him and not let go.

But she couldn't do it. He was going to break her heart.

He was playful with her now, attentive. But how long was that going to last? Until the next time she said no or didn't fit in with his schedule, or demanded what she knew he couldn't give her: a loving relationship.

She had to grow up and set some boundaries of her own.

'I want to be with you too, Alexei. But I think it's important to be pragmatic.'

'Pragmatic?' He didn't like the sound of that, although half an hour ago it had been exactly what he was after.

'When Kostya is settled I will need to go. It would be disastrous for him if he were to begin to think of us both as his parents—which is what would happen if…if I was in your life.' Maisy knew she was being sensible. She knew she was putting the interests of the child above her own, and she knew he couldn't argue with her on this. But, oh, she wished he would.

Alexei was silent. The playfulness had evaporated.

'He can't see us being…affectionate together in front of him,' she elaborated.

'Affectionate?'

'I know it's not really affection, I know it's just…sex. But he's so little he'll just see it as grown-ups showing love to each other, as we love him, and he'll think we all belong together.'

Alexei swore in Russian. Maisy blinked. His anger was evident, but it wasn't directed towards her. It was strange, but she sensed he was looking inward.

'I'm not an idiot, Alexei, I know how the world works. It's bizarre that we even met, let alone that I'm here. I think what's happened has happened because of the Kulikovs. We're both grieving and it gives us a bond. We've been thrown together, and it was…inevitable.'

'It *was* inevitable—I'll agree with that,' he replied, looking at her oddly. 'So what are your terms, Maisy?'

The question was blunt and to the point, and it hurt.

Terms? She had no idea. 'What—what usually happens when you're with a woman? I mean, how does it work?'

'I put her on the payroll and give her bonuses when she really performs.'

Maisy blinked again, and for an aching moment Alexei realised she wasn't sure if he was joking or not.

'Do you really think I'd do that? Listen.' He stood in front of her and tugged on her hands. 'That bed upstairs. It's mine. I don't bring women here. At all. Ever. This is my sanctuary.'

'No "female guests"?'

'Only a few, very firmly attached to their husbands. This is where I bring family.'

For a moment Maisy experienced an overwhelming explosion of belonging, even as common sense told her he was referring to Kostya. She was here because of Kostya. She wasn't a part of this family of his. But she was his first woman here.

'So what am I supposed to do?' She aimed for casual, but it came out needy.

Unexpectedly his thumb pressed against the frown line between her winged brows.

'Don't fret, Maisy. I'll make it easy for you. You live with me, you travel with me, you dodge the paparazzi with me. You'll be written up as "a mysterious redhead" until they dig out your details—and they will dig them up, dirt and all. Anything you want to keep hidden you can forget about. So, any bank robberies I need to know about?'

Maisy stared at him. Surely he was joking? No, not joking. 'Nobody will be interested in me. I'm not anybody.'

'Everything I do seems to attract some sort of interest. I'm hoping because you don't have a profile it will blow over.'

He'd thought about it. The realisation zoomed through Maisy's faltering confidence and made her feel a little stronger. Alexei had considered how she would fit into his life before now. Then she remembered all the security: in London, at the airport. Only here it seemed to have evaporated. It hadn't occurred to her before, but Alexei led a somewhat high-octane lifestyle.

What was that going to mean for her? More importantly, what would it mean for Kostya when she was gone? And she *would* go. She had told Alexei that much and he hadn't argued with her.

It made it easier for him. It made it terrifying for her.

He slid his big hands around her waist, sitting on the rim of the fountain and drawing her between his legs so that they were on eye level.

'Kostya is severely going to cramp our style,' he said, with a smile in his voice.

GET 2 BOOKS

We'd like to send you two *Harlequin Presents®* novels absolutely free. Accepting them puts you under no obligation to purchase any more books.

HOW TO GET YOUR 2 FREE BOOKS AND 2 FREE GIFTS

1. Return the reply card today, and we'll send you two *Harlequin Presents* novels, absolutely free! We'll even pay the postage!

2. Accepting free books places you under no obligation to buy anything, ever. Whatever you decide, the free books and gifts are yours to keep, free!

3. We hope that after receiving your free books you'll want to remain a subscriber, but the choice is yours– to continue or cancel, any time at all!

EXTRA BONUS

You'll also get two free mystery gifts! (worth about $10)

FREE!

'No, he's a wonderful little boy,' protested Maisy loyally. 'And he's so taken with you.'

'I agree wholeheartedly he's a great kid. But this "no affection" rule is going to be a bore.'

'There's no choice,' she said solemnly.

'There are always choices, *dushka*. You've exercised yours. Can you live by it?'

Maisy swayed into him. In his world there were choices—rich men always had choices. Unless by some miracle a leopard changed his spots and he fell head over heels in love with her…no, she didn't have a choice. She only had an inevitable outcome.

Alexei's arms came around her and he laid his head on the soft warm curve of her breasts. He released a lovely, deep, satisfied groan.

'What is it?' she asked, smiling at the sound.

'I've been wanting to do this all morning,' he revealed, looking up and flashing that killer smile. 'Your breasts are a gift to mankind. Well, to me—and at a stretch I'll share with Kostya.'

Maisy snorted and began to laugh.

'And now they're jiggling. I'm in heaven.'

'Stop it.' She smacked his shoulder lightly. 'You didn't answer my question before. Are you going to spend the rest of the day with Kostya?'

'Absolutely.'

'Can I have the day to myself?'

'You and Kostya?' he asked.

'No, I agree it's better if I'm not in the picture.'

Alexei set her back, hands linked behind her waist. 'There's a spa just outside of town. Why don't you spend the day there?'

Maisy didn't want to leave the circle of his arms, let alone go to a spa. But he was being sweet, offering her something she might like.

'I'll arrange it. A car will take you. What's that crease for?'

He gently smoothed her worry line with his thumb. 'What are you thinking now, little Maisy?'

'I don't know,' she said, suddenly breathless, wishing so much of this was different. If she had met him under different circumstances. If they had *courted*… Such an old-fashioned word. Maybe *dated* was better. She would have liked to be dated. Instead they'd set *terms*. 'I wish…'

'What do you wish?'

His voice had taken on that low timbre she liked so much, and her whole body began to speed up. *That we could be together, just the two of us, with no one else around.* 'I wish I had more clothes to wear,' she said instead, and that was true too. 'I think I'll go shopping.'

Alexei's arms released her. His expression was indulgent but somewhat cooler than what had been there earlier in his eyes. 'Excellent decision. Shop in the morning, spa in the afternoon.'

Maisy tried not to throw herself back into his arms. She couldn't very well pick up his hands and hold them on her waist. 'What will you do with Kostya?' she asked.

'Guy stuff.'

'He's two.'

'Guy stuff with training wheels,' he amended, and Maisy couldn't help smiling at the image. He really was trying with Kostya. It made her feel better about leaving him for the whole day.

'Whatever you do, remember to take his nappy bag and his water bottle. I'll pack it for you. And he needs his hat on at all times. He's so fair he burns in a trice.'

'I can do this.'

He suddenly looked so completely out of his depth that Maisy couldn't help herself, and launched herself into his arms. She wrapped her arms around his neck and inhaled the lovely male smell of him that she would keep with her for the rest of the day.

Alexei's hands landed gingerly on her waist, as if he was

startled by her sudden missile launch of affection. 'I'm hugging you,' she told him, her voice muffled by his shoulder. His arms tightened around her nicely and Maisy smiled contentment.

Alexei frowned into the middle distance. He hadn't expected any of this: the time it was going to take to build a bond with Leo's little boy, the emotional investment. Yet what choice did he have? There were two other couples waiting in the wings to take responsibility for him; it would perhaps be the most sensible course to hand the boy over to one of them. Yet Leo had named *him* Kostya's guardian. Leo didn't do anything without a reason, and Alexei didn't back down from a challenge.

But he hadn't expected Maisy, who was presenting her own unique challenge.

The minute they'd hit the bed this morning every one of his tightly held tenets about women and sex had flown out of the window. It was probably to do with her innocence, which was playing havoc with the traditional Russian male he'd thought he'd done a good job of burying deep enough that he hadn't thought about marriage and children and a future in years. Not since he'd made his first million and women had become easy and their expectations primarily mercenary.

Maisy, with her long glossy ringlets tickling his chest and her soft sweet mouth trading slow kisses, eyes shut, expression dreamy, as if he was every one of her fantasies rolled into one, had seemed much more absorbed in making this morning romantic than in the sort of sexual marathon it turned into. That was *his* doing. He hadn't been able to get enough of her. Her subsequent reaction to him meant he'd have to be deaf, dumb and blind not to realise she was investing her emotions in this, in *him*. But what was confusing him was that he was virtually *encouraging* it.

He'd put it down to the ego-stroke of having a woman more interested in his attention than his bank balance, but he knew he had to put matters on a more fiscal level. Once he was keeping her the whole aura of romance would dissolve, and the little touches of sweetness, her insecurity about his feelings, would be smoothed over by regular cheques.

Hell, the sheets upstairs were barely cool and she was planning a shopping trip. Maisy was a sweet girl, and she was heat itself between the sheets, but at the end of the day why should she be any different from anyone else? And why was he even entertaining notions of what it would be like if she was?

Feeling as if she had run an emotional marathon, Maisy came down the main stairs, checking her purse. Credit card, passport, the Italian currency she had bought yesterday. She was all set to go shopping, and she wouldn't be a card-carrying woman if the thought of a few hours looking at clothes didn't pique her interest. The added bonus of a little pampering this afternoon put a smile on her face.

Alexei had made an appointment for her in a spa in the hills at two, giving her a few hours to trawl the shops. Andrei would be driving her, which was the best news she'd had. All Maisy wanted to do was prop herself up at a window, watch the scenery drift by and daydream like a teenage girl about Alexei. She knew it was silly, but she hadn't been able to think of anything else but him since he'd burst into that kitchen at Lantern Square. Now her thoughts had a vivid sexual imagery that scorched her cheeks but kept a little smile triggered on her lips.

She was smiling as she reached the mezzanine and Carlo Santini came out of nowhere. She hadn't realised he was even on the premises, but given the size of the place that was probably a moot point.

'Miss Edmonds?'

Maisy tried not to look worried.

'Alexei asked me to pass on these items to you. This is the security key that gives access to all areas of the villa. If you ever require a motor car, as you do today, there will be a driver always at your disposal. Just phone through to the house office and it will be arranged. Here is the number.'

He held out a smart phone and unwillingly she took it. She had no idea how to use it.

'An account has been opened in your name. Here are the details, and your cards.'

'A bank account?'

'Si.' He smiled at her then, and she didn't like his smile. 'Did you think you would not be paid, *signorina*?'

Maisy's whole being ground to a halt. She remained silent. His smile was definitely not pleasant. She hadn't imagined that.

'Now is your chance to spend up, Miss Edmonds. Mr Ranaevsky is a very generous man.'

Maisy stayed where she was a long time after Carlo had left her, the smart phone heavy in her hands. She looked at the clear plastic wallet of cards through a blur of tears.

It was *stupid* to be angry, stupid to be hurt. This was how he did things. This was what she had agreed to. But knowing that and really *understanding* that she wasn't special, she was just part of the way he ran his life—his empire—bit hard.

He was showing her very clearly the *terms*.

But Carlo Santini had looked at her as if she were some sort of woman to be paid off.

Those weren't *her* terms.

Shoving everything into her handbag, she barrelled down the remaining flight of stairs. She'd show him. She wouldn't spend a *cent* of his stupid money.

Four hours later Maisy was blissfully prone under the experienced hands of a masseuse, all the knots and tension in her muscles worked away. She hadn't realised how much she had needed this—not just the massage, but time away by herself. And she didn't feel guilty—not about leaving Kostya, who was in safe hands, nor about this morning and what she and Alexei had done in that big bed. Twenty-four hours ago she would have had a hard time disrobing for a massage, but now she was lying naked on her belly, a towel draped discreetly over her lower body, content to be pummelled and oiled and taken care of.

What a difference a day made—or rather a very satisfying morning.

Bundled in a white robe, her hair wrapped in a treatment, Maisy thumbed through a pile of glossy magazines, her thoughts on what she should wear home from her new purchases. She wanted Alexei to see the full impact of the results all this pampering yielded, but mostly it would be so lovely to just feel beautiful. There hadn't been much time or space in the past two years for feeling beautiful.

She flipped a page in the social events section of a glossy US magazine and her thoughts came to a stuttering stop.

It was Alexei. He was on a boat, at a party, his arm around the waist of Tara Mills. Maisy didn't have to read the caption to recognise her face. It had been on a billboard at Naples airport when they'd flown in. More than a model, she was a brand.

Finding it difficult to draw in enough air, Maisy began to read the paragraph below.

Has Tara met her match in Alexei Ranaevsky, Russian oligarch and all-round bad boy? If the diamonds around her neck are anything to go by, Ranaevsky is serious.

It wasn't the silly words penned by a journalist that froze Maisy, it was the reality of Alexei's past that threw her. Alexei had dated Tara Mills?

Calm down, she told herself, tossing the magazine aside. He was allowed to have a past. But she couldn't help it. She picked up another and started flipping through to the social pages, and then another. Alexei was everywhere, arm around a different woman, all of them with skyscraper cheekbones, mile-long legs and the attitude to go with it. Blondes, brunettes—it didn't seem to matter.

I'm the redhead.

He had told her about this—that his life was the subject of

media scrutiny, that she would be written up, that there would be little privacy—and she hadn't paid enough attention. Well, she was paying attention now. She was looking at the evidence of exactly *why* Alexei was a media darling. He was wealthy and powerful and gorgeous, and he paraded women like the sports cars she had seen lined up in the converted stables at the villa.

How on earth has this happened to me?

Not in a million years had she ever imagined this would be a lifestyle she would be stepping into. She took a good look around her. She had wondered over the cost of this spa treatment when she'd stepped from the car and been greeted by an attendant, and been impressed by the luxury surrounds— another converted villa—but had not fully appreciated how exclusive the spa might be. This was a spa with guests—virtually a hotel—and given she was the only client in the facilities she had a fair idea that personalised, discreet service for wealthy patrons was the name of the game.

Without even realising it she had landed in a fantasy. Except it wasn't *her* fantasy. She didn't want to be photographed and written about. Not that there was anything to write other than *Alexei Ranaevsky slums it with naive redhead.*

Maisy felt as if a huge lump had taken up residence in her throat. Even after her hair was blow-dried to glossy silk, her nails French polished and her face delicately enhanced with some colour, she looked in the mirror and all she saw was a fool.

Maisy was home.

Alexei brought his conference call to a grinding halt, leaving a shocked Carlo Santini to mop up the mess. Every sensible cell in his head was telling him to let her come to him, but every instinct was dragging him down those stairs.

He found her standing in the entrance hall, surrounded by shopping bags—a couple from boutiques he vaguely recognised, the rest clearly retail.

'Bravo.' He stopped on the bottom step and commenced a slow hand-clap. 'You've bought out the Amalfi Coast.'

Maisy looked up, and for a moment she didn't say a word. She just looked at him as if she was seeing him for the first time. Then a parody of a smile broke out on her pink-painted lips and she said, 'I should be exhausted, but I'm not. I had so much fun.'

Her enthusiasm was so palpably false Alexei just waited for the punchline.

It didn't come. She began gathering up some of her bags and Andrei, who had driven her around all day, scooped up the rest, earning one of Maisy's sunny artless smiles. Alexei found himself crossing the floor rapidly, intervening, deciding on the spot to organise a different driver to transport Maisy around. He didn't like the way the younger man's eyes lingered on Maisy's face. He'd be sprawled on the floor if that gaze moved anywhere else on her body.

Maisy preceded him up the stairs—at least her bottom hadn't changed. Shapely, still moving like a pendulum when she walked, then charged ahead to the nursery, almost running from him.

He'd fix that.

'I've shifted your room.'

Maisy slowed, turned. She looked distinctly disturbed.

'I had no idea you were sleeping in a broom closet. I've put you in the room next to mine. The one I slept in last night.'

'Oh.' Maisy looked as if she'd wanted to say something but had thought better of it.

'But you'll be sleeping in my bed,' he added.

On receipt of that little announcement Maisy clung on to her shopping bags like life rafts. What in the hell was the matter with her?

'Is that a problem?

'No,' she said stiffly, 'of course not.'

Clearly it was. 'I didn't think it would be.' He didn't mean to sound clipped, but she was already moving away from him, heels clicking. She really had the most endearing walk in heels—as if she hadn't quite mastered them.

Maisy kept going. If she could just get to her room and shut the door, get herself together before she had to face him again, it would be all right. But he was undoing her with every word.

Of course he followed her into her room. She wasn't going to get any time alone. With her head in overdrive, she was wondering just how she could bring up the spectre of a million other women and not sound like a jealous shrew?

'Can I have a minute?' she asked, her voice light and thin.

'I haven't seen you all day, Maisy. Didn't you miss me?' He had closed the door and was leaning back against it, all lean, muscular grace. His stunning blue eyes were not on her, however. They were on the bags.

The room had a whole wall of glass facing onto a terrace. The view was breathtaking. But Maisy turned her back to the water, setting down her bags on the floor. 'I haven't had much time to miss you,' she replied stiffly. 'I was so busy. Did you have a lovely day with Kostya?'

He gave her a tight smile, and she realised her odd behaviour was impacting on him. He pushed away from the door, coming towards her with an intent that made her step back. If he touched her now she would hit him. He merely dumped her bags on the bed.

'You *have* been a busy girl. A complete wardrobe overhaul?'

'No,' Maisy said slowly, 'just a few new dresses. I packed for Paris, not Italy, and it's very warm, and I thought—' She broke off, wondering why she was explaining herself to him.

Defending herself.

'I got Kostya some overalls and the sweetest pair of pyjamas,' she barrelled on, determined to steer the subject into more neutral waters.

She caught her breath as Alexei snagged a lingerie carrier.

Suddenly, knowing what she did and in this mood, she didn't want him to see her purchases. She had made them when she felt loved-up, and she was feeling distinctly frozen out right now. Amazing what being at the end of a long line of sensationally attractive women did for an ordinary girl's ego.

'No—don't,' she said, reaching for the bag. But he whipped it out of her reach.

'You can't disappoint me now, *dushka*. I mean, you hardly made this little purchase for yourself.'

And he shook out all the frilly nothings she had indulged in over the bed.

He zeroed in on an ivory satin negligee with lace inserts. Maisy put a hand to her temple. She could hardly pretend now she hadn't made these purchases for him.

Alexei didn't know what he'd expected to find. The satin slid through his fingers like water. It was a classic negligee. His gaze went to the bra-and-knicker sets on the bed. All classy, in pale colours. Nothing outrageous, nothing overtly sexy—everything to remind him Maisy had been wearing plain white knickers with just a bit of lace this morning.

Suddenly he knew he'd blundered. He couldn't see a price tag on any of this, he just saw understated elegance, and he was given the strong impression of a woman who had come into his life without any intention of seducing a man. He could have told her all she needed to do was smile at him and he was hers.

'I like this,' he said gruffly.

'I don't think they have it in your size,' Maisy said tartly, surprising him, reaching out and snatching it out of his hand. She added assertively, 'I didn't buy this for you. I bought it for me.'

He smiled slowly, watched the wariness in her eyes turn into something else—something closer to where they had been first thing this morning. He liked it when she was like this: ready to stand up for herself, willing to take him on. Few people did it in his world. He liked it when it was the woman in his bed.

Which reminded him. 'Wear it tonight,' he said, more abruptly than he'd meant.

She frowned. 'Is that an order or a request?'

'And wear your hair down,' he said, as if she hadn't spoken, crowding her. He couldn't help himself. She smelled like sandalwood and bergamot, and that indefinable Maisy-smell he'd had tattooed on his skin this morning.

Maisy opened her mouth to give him a piece of her mind, but he picked up one of her ringlets and bussed the end of her nose with it.

'Don't look so dire, Maisy. It's just sex.' And with that he bent and brushed his mouth over hers, effectively silencing her.

She tried to tell herself he *hadn't* just given her the real terms of their arrangement, but something curdled deep in her belly. First the money, and then all those other women. She would never mention the other women to him—she had too much pride—but by God she would tackle him over the money.

She pushed her hands up against his chest and gave him a shove.

'Maisy?'

He actually sounded disconcerted. She shook her head disbelievingly. 'I thought we'd sorted this out. I thought we had an arrangement.'

'Okay.' He backed up. 'What's the problem? You've been like a cat on a hot tin roof since we got up here.'

'You put me on your damn payroll. I thought it was a joke, but it's not. You got that awful Carlo Santini to give me money!'

'I'm not allowed to spend money on you?'

'You're not spending money on me. You're *paying* me.' She shook her head. He just didn't get it. 'And for your information I have my own money.'

'No doubt. But life is going to get expensive for you, Maisy. You're with me now.'

'Am I?' She doubted that. The problem was she didn't feel as if she was *with* him—and how could she after a single day? She felt like a fraud. The girl who *accidentally* ended up in Alexei Ranaevsky's bed whilst he was on vacation from his models and his actresses and his Euro trash. She added the last to make herself feel a little better.

Alexei closed in on her again, his hands closing over her arms. 'Don't make it a big deal, Maisy. Let's just play it as it goes.'

'You think less of me because I've never held down a job,' she blurted out, not sure what she was saying any more.

'Where did that come from?' He angled a frown at her.

'You said so last night—'

'I said a lot of things last night, *dushka*. I want you to forget them and just focus on the here and now.'

'I have a job. Looking after Kostya,' she ploughed on, refusing to be diverted. 'And I can tell you, caring for a young child is a hundred times more difficult than buying up companies or cruising the stockmarket or whatever it is you do!'

Alexei's mouth quirked at Maisy's dismissive summing up of his hard-won business empire.

'I agree,' he said. 'It is more difficult and in a completely different way. But I'm here now. That life is over, Maisy. Time to let it go and face up to a few facts of life.'

'Facts? Such as?'

'Life has changed for you. The horizon has widened. Your little purse, *dushka*, isn't going to bear the strain.' He smiled slowly, his eyes stroking her. 'Let me spoil you, Maisy.'

That line usually worked a treat.

Maisy's mouth formed an ominous little line. 'Does that mean I get a diamond necklace?'

Alexei's eyes hardened, his hands falling away from her. 'You've been reading the tabloids.'

'No, just upmarket magazines. You're a bit hard to miss.'

'Is that what this is all about? Don't you think that's a bit beneath us, *dushka*?'

He actually sounded impatient. Maisy's temper went into overdrive.

'You're a real piece of work, aren't you?' she exploded, giving him a good shove, frustrated that even when she put all her effort behind it she couldn't shift him an inch. 'A different girl for every day of the week. Well, I'm not going to be one of them, Alexei. I have my own money. I have my own jewellery. All I want from you is—' She broke off, scrambling for a neutral term.

'*Da*? What is it you want from me, Maisy?'

'Sex,' she snapped. 'To quote you. *Just sex.*'

'Now we're talking.' His gaze did a run of her body.

Maisy stiffened all over. She couldn't imagine what he saw in her. And that was the problem. She knew it was her own insecurities—but, damn it, why couldn't his former women-friends be a little less polished, a little more…ordinary?

But she was looking at the reason why. Spectacular bone structure, height, lean muscular build and a mind like a steel trap. He was a prize. But not one granted to girls like her. It was on the tip of her tongue to ask him why. But that would have been too humiliating.

He in turn was studying her like a puzzle. She backed away from him and began shoving the underwear back into the carrier, refusing to look at him. She felt like such a fool, going to all this effort to look pretty for him, spending money she couldn't afford on lingerie that was probably laughably tame compared to what he was used to.

Out of her depth didn't even cover it. *Don't make it a big deal.* Those were his words. Because it clearly wasn't a big deal to him.

'I'm convinced I should have tied you to the bed this morning,' Alexei muttered, expression shuttered.

Maisy turned her back on him and marched into the wardrobe. When she re-emerged he was gone.

Just sex, he'd said. So now she knew.

CHAPTER EIGHT

MAISY was almost done feeling sorry for herself, but her shoulder was starting to ache and it was making her tetchy. She told herself all she wanted was to crawl into bed—her own bed. But that wasn't what she had signed up for. She had Kostya to bathe and read to and put to bed, and then it would be time to front up to entertain the man who put diamonds around the neck of Tara Mills. Mr *Don't Make It A Big Deal*.

But it was a big deal. She just knew she wasn't going to be able to get past the knowledge of all those other women. Not because of who they were—each individual blurred into one glossy, silicone-enhanced mass—but because it made no sense at all why he was with her now.

She kicked off her heels and padded barefoot to the nursery. It was after six, and Kostya was fractious after his long and exciting day. He babbled about ponies and kept mentioning another boy, one of Maria's grandsons, but mainly he talked about 'Alessi', who was clearly a big hit. As he should be, Maisy thought wearily as she ran his bath and collected the assortment of plastic toys he required.

He was splashing and Maisy was wilting when Alexei put in his appearance, hair damp, freshly shaved, smelling faintly of luxury cologne and male skin. Maisy was suddenly immensely grateful she had spent her afternoon being doused in oils and potions that gave her hair and skin a gleaming intensity her sinking spirits did not match.

The immediate rapport between man and boy sent her into

the corner, perching on the washing hamper, whilst Alexei conducted the Royal Navy in the bathtub.

'I'll put him to bed,' Alexei assured her over his shoulder. 'Go and fix yourself up and I'll fetch you for dinner.'

Fix yourself up. Maisy eyed the soap dish. Could she crack his skull with it if she applied enough force?

'Maisy?'

'I heard,' she said, not bothering to disguise the irritation in her voice.

What in the hell was wrong with her now? Alexei watched as she leaned down to kiss Kostya's downy curls, her ringlets sliding forward. She was very sweet with him. He found himself leaning forward as Kostya reached up and tugged on one of her curls and held on.

Alexei saw a flash of the old Maisy, laughing a little as she detached herself from Kostya's tenacious grip. He hadn't fully realised she had gone until she'd laughed, her expression softening.

It threw him. He'd been so busy justifying his own behaviour he'd forgotten this sweetness, this warmth that had drawn him in to begin with. He wanted this Maisy back—the one who had greeted him at his bedroom door in just his shirt; the one who had wrapped her arms around him this morning in the garden.

If Kostya wasn't here he'd have her stripped and gasping under him on the bathroom tiles, all arguments and all anxieties over how she'd fit in his life erased by mind-blowing sex. But mind-blowing sex wasn't going to fix the problem with Maisy, because the problem *was* the mind-blowing sex. She had blindsided him this morning. Last night he'd planned a practised seduction, a little recreational sex with a pretty girl. He could actually pinpoint the moment it had stopped being familiar territory and started being something entirely new: when she'd leaned into his car and told him she wasn't going to do as he told him and powered off with that pram, a swing in her hips. She said no at every turn, to a man who rarely if ever heard the word and when he did, manoeuvred his way around it. She'd been defying him ever since, going her own way even when it left her trapped on a terrace or spending money she probably didn't have on lingerie to seduce him.

So he'd sent Carlo to her with that credit card. He'd arranged a bank account for her. He'd done all he could to force her to conform to the stereotype he'd constructed to *handle* the women in his life. To neutralise relationships.

If he'd planned to push her away he couldn't have done any better.

He caught hold of her hand as she straightened up and she looked startled. He pressed his lips to her palm. It was a gesture designed to reassure her, but her eyes just flared wide— as if she thought he was going to launch himself at her here and now.

Irritation at the gulf between his expectations and her experience must have made itself known in his expression, because she jerked her hand free as if he'd scalded her.

Releasing a deep sigh, Alexei said, 'It shouldn't be this hard, *dushka*.'

Maisy tried not to load his words with meaning, but as she dressed she couldn't douse the suspicion that she'd managed this afternoon to severely damage whatever connection they'd had in bed that morning.

She stood in front of the mirror, checking herself from all angles in her heels and her new underwear. The image in the mirror was disconcerting. A taller, voluptuous, sex kitten Maisy. The one she'd known existed deep in her fantasy life but who had never been given the kit to play dress-up in and come into being. She hadn't really bought this underwear for him, she realized. It was for herself. To make her feel confident.

Everything she had done this morning, everything Alexei had done to her, played itself over in Technicolor as she lifted her black satin dress over her head. It slid like water down her body and she felt her pulse leap lightly as her silhouette metamorphosed with the aid of her expensive lingerie.

I look good, she thought, feeling more confident. She carefully ran a brush through her ringlets, slicked her lips with the glittery lipstick she had purchased at the spa. They looked fuller, and with her eyes made up she looked as beautiful as she had felt this morning, when Alexei had been moving inside her and she'd had his whole rapt attention.

That was what she missed, she realised, and she didn't know how to get it back. She was puzzling over it when a rap on her door broke the spell.

Alexei was leaning on the wall across the hall from her door. He was dressed up. Dinner shirt, jacket and dark pants. Muscles and testosterone and moody blue eyes. Maisy's pulse picked up, overriding the morass of feeling that was swamping her tonight. She almost forgot how different she looked, but was reminded as Alexei came away from the wall, his sullen mouth widening into a decidedly elemental smile.

He said something in Russian. It sounded beautiful—all rolling 'r's and hushed vowels. Then he said something else, and it sounded dirty.

'Suddenly I don't have an appetite,' he finally said in English, crowding her. 'Let's skip the food and get down to business.'

She closed the door quietly behind her, then folded her arms in a self-protective gesture that wiped the smile off Alexei's face.

'I was joking, Maisy. The helicopter's waiting. We've got a table booked.'

'We're going out?'

'It's usually the idea when you dine with a beautiful woman.'

Natural colour swept into her cheeks and Alexei relaxed. He watched her arms unfold, some of the tension flow out of her shoulders and her spine lift.

'I can't believe we're going out in public,' she marvelled. 'On a proper date, like normal people.'

Alexei stared at her, wondering if she was actually going to clap her hands and jump up and down.

'Except for the helicopter,' she added, smiling.

'I can do normal,' he asserted roughly. He was starting to get the hint that what worked for Maisy were the traditional aspects of relations between men and women. He could do that. He suddenly wondered if he should have brought her flowers. Instead he obeyed a sudden instinct and bent and kissed her gently on the cheek, took her hand.

Maisy lit up like Christmas in response, and floated after him.

Afterwards she didn't know where she'd found the nerve to climb into the glass fishbowl he called a helicopter, but she got to cling to him in the dark, which made it all worthwhile.

It was a magical night. The exclusive restaurant was in Naples, and Maisy would never forget slipping out of the limo with Alexei and walking hand in hand the rest of the way through the old city. They had a private room, but Maisy had the thrill of walking across a room full of people on his arm. She discovered she had an appetite, despite her long and eventful day, stealing bits off Alexei's plate and feeding him the anchovies she couldn't stand. As she licked up her dessert—a meringue and cream fantasy with tiny pink crystals that melted on her tongue—she knew for once exactly what she needed to do tonight to make everything perfect.

Alexei had brandy and coffee, watching her eat with obvious pleasure. She extended her spoon to him and he obliged, taking a sweet mouthful he didn't want just to make her smile.

'I don't want this night to end,' she confided as he draped her cape around her shoulders.

'Would you like to go dancing?'

Maisy turned up happy eyes. 'I would.'

Alexei took her to a supper club where he could slow dance with her. Maisy wrapped her arms around him, wanting to tell him this was the first time she'd danced like this. He was her first in so many ways. She shivered in reaction.

'What is it, *dushka*?'

His voice had dropped to a low pitch that thrummed in her belly.

Speaking before she could lose her nerve, she replied, 'I want to make love with you.'

She actually felt Alexei's breath hitch in his chest beneath the press of her hand. It was gratifying, and thrilling. For the first time since they'd met she felt as if she had taken the reins.

'Shall we go home?' she suggested.

Alexei didn't argue.

Something had altered. Maisy felt the change come over Alexei as they entered the house. All the lights were glittering in the many windows, and the place looked like a fairytale castle, but Alexei strode across the mezzanine and up the stairs as if on a mission.

Maisy struggled along behind, no longer holding his hand but being shackled and dragged. So much for taking the reins. But she didn't mind all that much. If he wanted to behave like a caveman she was happy to be what he was dragging back to his cave.

To her annoyance, Carlo Santini stepped out of the corridor at the top of the stairs. Alexei swore when he saw him. A volley of vitriolic Russian intruded on Maisy's dreamy state.

Alexei made a silencing gesture with one hand, then turned with elaborate politeness and said in English, 'A small emergency has arisen, Maisy. I may be some time.'

He didn't touch her. He didn't kiss her. He just walked away. And Maisy, disappointment settling over her, very slowly bent down and removed her shoes, sinking back down to ground level.

In her stockinged feet she returned to her room. She felt alarmingly keyed-up, but had no intention of decking herself out on his bed on the faint chance he would return and want her on tap. The moment had passed.

She didn't know why, but seeing Carlo Santini had reminded

her of the type of relationship Alexei had set down for them. He had his life, his work—which he was now attending to— and he had a woman for recreation. Which happened to be her.

It didn't go a long way to making a girl feel special.

Maisy stripped herself of all her clothes but didn't take a shower. She spent a long time scrubbing her make-up off until she was barefaced. She hesitated over the negligee. Something was niggling—something that told her if she donned it and waited for him she would be playing right into his stupid mistress scenario.

So she dug out her old sleepshirt instead. It was just a long white T-shirt with a cartoon mouse on the front, soft from hundreds of washings. It felt so familiar she was assailed with an overwhelming longing for a simpler life, and the less complicated girl she had once been.

I need Anais, she thought sadly, curling up like a snail on her bed. Anais would read Alexei like a book and provide footnotes. *To me he's just a seething mass of testosterone and conflicting messages. I can't keep up.* She yawned and snuggled into her pillow, hugging it to her. Her bed felt huge and empty, but it wasn't as if she wasn't used to sleeping alone.

She surfaced to consciousness with a sigh. A large male hand was on her inner thigh and she jolted, rolling backwards to thud into his big, solid body.

'Alexei. You gave me a fright,' she mumbled groggily.

'I apologise, *dushka*, I didn't mean to wake you.' But he was kissing the back of her neck in the way she'd learned she liked, and her bottom was pressed against what was clearly on his mind.

'I can't do this,' she protested, but he was already lifting her T-shirt, peeling it up her body. She squirmed and pulled away. 'No, stop it.' She kicked out at him. 'I need to sleep.'

'Sleep?' Alexei sounded incredulous.

'Yes,' she muttered. 'And so do you if your mood's anything to go by.'

A very big part of her wanted him to pull her into his arms

and override her objections. Instead Alexei literally thrust himself away from her, rolling onto his back, sweeping aside the covers.

'Where are you going?' she demanded softly, struggling to sit up.

He jack-knifed out of the bed. 'I need a shower, if that's all right by you. A cold one.'

Maisy pulled the covers back over her, but as the minutes went by she felt herself shivering. It only grew worse as the time ticked by. She heard the shower being switched on and off. Any minute now he was going to walk through here and out of that door.

She heard the door open, shut. Maisy rolled over to watch him in the moonlight coming through the window. He was picking up her clothes.

'What are you doing?' she framed softly.

He didn't reply. He draped her gown over the armchair in the corner, and then her bra, her stockings and barely there cami-knickers. All the bits she had strewn carelessly over the floor. Maisy had never met a coat hanger she liked.

She watched him silently, still shivering but feeling strangely moved. His gestures were so precise they seemed to have meaning. Now he would leave, she thought, as he ran out of items. Except he didn't. He climbed into bed beside her and there was only the sound of his breathing, steady and deep, and hers, uncertain and shallow.

'Your emergency,' she said uncertainly. 'What was it about?'

Alexei was silent for so long Maisy didn't think he was going to answer her. His words startled her when he did speak. 'It was to do with a timber company.'

'Nothing serious?' She had an excuse now to roll over.

Alexei was lying on his back, naked, one arm hooked behind his head. He was staring up at the ceiling and didn't look at her, but she could see the tiredness in the set of his profile and for the first time it occurred to her how work never stopped for him.

'I've dealt with the bare necessities. There's nothing that can't be cleared up tomorrow.'

She realised he had left things unresolved to return to her. Before she could enjoy the feeling she remembered Carlo Santini. She remembered all the women.

Yet here he was, in bed with her.

Maisy drew the covers more securely around her neck. She was so cold, and it wasn't going away. She felt cold to the bone.

'I had an amazing time tonight,' she said quietly into the dark. 'I want to thank you.'

Alexei's head shifted. His eyes welded with hers. 'You were happy,' he said. It wasn't a question, it was a statement. Then he frowned. 'You're shivering.'

His whole body shifted then. He lifted the covers and literally dragged her into him, and she was engulfed in Alexei. Cold shower or not, his body was like the sun. He exuded heat and comfort, but she couldn't relax.

'Talk to me,' he murmured into her hair. 'Tell me about how you came to be at the Kulikovs'.' When she was silent he prompted, 'You met Anais at school?'

Maisy didn't want to go near the Anais and Leo question. He had reacted so strongly the other night she didn't want to risk it. But with her cheek pressed against his firm, warm chest she felt a little safer to talk about it. It wasn't as if he'd tip her out of bed, would he?

'Anais came to St Bernice's when we were fourteen. She was a skinny beanpole and I was a chubby little swot.' She said it lightly, but it was forced.

Alexei smoothed his palm over the curve of her hip. Maisy felt something inside give a little, because he'd made it extremely clear since they'd met that the womanly aspects of her body were what he found desirable.

'You were close?'

'I was bullied a little, because I wasn't from the right sort of background, and Anais fought those battles for me. I'll always be grateful to her for that.'

'So what happened at the end of school?'

'Anais went modelling and I—' Maisy took a deep breath. She had never told a soul this story and it felt strange doing so now. But the dark helped—and the heavy solidity of Alexei wrapped around her. 'My mum got sick. I looked after her.'

'I see.'

But he didn't see. He couldn't know what a slow descent those two years had been. She'd been on the verge of her adult life and it had all been taken away.

'Your mother is dead.' He said it bluntly.

Maisy looked up at him. 'How do you know? Oh, the investigators.' She tried to put a little room between them but he refused to let her budge.

'No, I didn't get them to dig that far. I know because you haven't made any phone calls to England. All girls call their mothers at some point.'

'Even if my mum was alive I probably wouldn't be ringing her,' said Maisy frankly.

'She did a job on you?' He propped himself up so he could watch her telltale face.

'She was a single mum. She was only sixteen when she had me. She always told me I'd ruined her life. Then she got cancer and she needed me.'

Alexei rubbed his thumb over the pulse at the base of her throat. 'Then what happened?'

'I ran into Anais in a department store in London. It was just weeks after Mum's funeral. I was—numb. And suddenly there she was. She was pregnant with Kostya and she wanted me to move in with her and help. She didn't have any sisters and her mum was a bit of a nightmare.'

'You had that in common.' He was brushing the hair out of her eyes. She loved it when he did that, felt cherished by him. 'And you stayed with her thereafter?'

Maisy was silent. She suddenly felt tremulous. He was straying very close to dangerous ground.

'You never thought about going back to school?'

If there was an implied criticism in there she couldn't detect it, and it gave her the courage to answer honestly. 'After Mum died I thought about university. I'd got in, but I couldn't go because of Mum. And then Anais appeared and I made my decision. I can't regret it.'

'Surely Leo could have got you a job in one of his companies? I know you, Maisy. You're a smart girl.'

It wasn't the use of the description 'smart' that pleased her. It was the assertion *I know you.* He didn't, but the assurance he had that he did made her feel warm inside. Wanted.

'I had a baby to look after. It doesn't give you much room for a social life, let alone a job.'

'So tell me about this one lover, one time.'

He spoke so casually, just slipped it in, his fingers sliding gently through one of her long curls. But Maisy wasn't fooled. He was marking his ground.

Maisy *really* didn't want to discuss Dan with Alexei. It made her feel pathetic, and she desperately didn't want him to see her as that.

'Were you in a relationship with him?'

'Of course I was,' Maisy answered unthinkingly, then stiffened. She had jumped into bed with Alexei quickly enough, and this wasn't anything like a relationship. There was no *of course* about it. She waited for him to react, but he was observing her as if what she was saying was fascinating. 'I don't really want to discuss it,' she said quietly. 'It happened. That's it.'

'You were in a relationship, you lost your virginity and that was it? No repeat performance?'

'I called it quits.' Suddenly the stitching on the edge of the bedsheet became the most interesting thing in the room.

'How long were you seeing each other?'

'Six weeks.'

'So a long-term thing?'

Maisy felt her temper stir and lift. 'Okay, you've made your point. I'm not sophisticated, and I had crappy sex with a crappy boy in his crappy bedsit. But look—now I've come up in the world. Better sex with a better boy in a better bed.'

'Better sex?' He chuckled, the sound a gravitational pull that had her edging back in against him. 'This is fantastic sex, *dushka*. The best I've ever had.'

Maisy spun for a moment on that assertion. He couldn't be serious?

'And for your information, Maisy,' he murmured, his breath warm in her ear, 'I'm not a boy. I'm a man. And there's a difference.'

Maisy knew that. Alexei had made it very clear what that difference was since day one.

'I wish I'd known you then,' he inserted softly.

'You wouldn't have given me the time of day.'

There—she'd said it. Her throat was aching with unexpressed emotions she was finding it difficult to keep repressed.

She felt the change in Alexei's body and it was like a kick to her belly. He didn't want to hear her insecurities, but they were all she felt tonight. The day had been too volatile; too much had happened to her. And now she couldn't sleep. She could only lie pinned to him, baring her soul to a man who probably wanted nothing less.

'I would have taken you to a luxurious hotel and taken your virginity with a great deal more care than some bloke in a bedsit,' he said with rough assurance.

Maisy pressed her temple against his chest. For a moment she allowed herself to believe him. He was touching her, his palms and fingertips moving over her waist and back and hips in circular movements, but not in a sexual way. At least she didn't think so. He was just warming her.

'Alexei…' she murmured.

'Hmm?'

'I wish it had been you,' she confessed. 'I know we're just having a fling. But I wish it had been you.'

Alexei's hands had stopped moving and it felt as if he'd stopped breathing.

'It's how I feel,' she said nervously, wondering what the stillness meant.

His big hand tipped her chin up and he brought his mouth down on hers, hard and hot and possessive. She had the fleeting thought, *This is just like London.* And it rocked her.

His hands were suddenly under her T-shirt and around her breasts. Maisy felt her body rev to speed without a second thought. She was still shivering, but she couldn't *not* respond. He was still hers. She could already feel him at her core, and she was wet for him. He tore her old shirt in two, baring her breasts. He entered her with a single thrust and she rocked into him, not caring about anything but the fury that was driving her upwards. She'd gone from virtually zero in the physical department to Alexei's level in the span of a day. God knew what he had created. Maisy didn't even know who she was any more.

She splintered into a thousand pieces so quickly she could have wept, but he was still moving in her, and Maisy clung to him, digging her nails into the slabs of muscle behind his shoulders, feeling it build again. His mouth kept contact with hers, his eyes pinning her so that when she climaxed again he was with her. But it was different this time. She felt him pour himself into her. Sweat glistened on his shoulders where Maisy pressed her mouth, and then he was sinking heavily on top of her. He stayed inside her, not moving. Her heartbeat began to thrum to the rhythm of his and she closed her eyes, the tears rising and choking her.

'It's not a fling,' he muttered. Then he lifted himself up on his forearms and fixed her face in place with his hands. He meshed their mouths. 'It's not a fling,' he repeated.

Just in case she hadn't heard him the first time.

Alexei gave Kostya his promised three days. He introduced him to the sea, held his tiny barrel-shaped body in the gently breaking surf as it creamed the shore and built sandcastles for the sea to destroy.

Maisy sheltered under a huge hat and a billowy sheer

shirt—the sun had never been kind to her—and feasted her eyes on Alexei in a pair of low-slung board shorts that did nothing to curb her X-rated thoughts. His golden tan made a mockery of her pale, lightly freckled skin. She could blame the heat of the day for her hot flush as he strode up the beach to where she sat under an umbrella, her trashy novel fluttering in the breeze, but his gaze told her otherwise, locking on the sumptuous curves of her breasts and hips in the flattering fifties-style bikini.

Last night had shifted something in their relationship. The tensions between them seemed to have evaporated, and on this private beach, in the full glare of the late-afternoon sun, Maisy felt an enormous clutch of contentment and the wicked stir of her body. It was as if her body was suddenly fully awake after a long sleep, and like Sleeping Beauty she was in thrall to her prince. Her gloriously built prince, with his slumberous smile and Tartar eyes eating her up as she fumbled in her bag for sunscreen to reapply to Kostya's sand-encrusted nose.

It was her rule that they shouldn't show physical affection in front of Kostya, but it was a rule she was regretting as six and a half feet of Russian male stretched himself out on the lounger beside her, his long, lean body glistening with seawater and sand, his lashes wet and black, framing his brilliant eyes. He lay there watching her, looking immensely relaxed and happy. The grim, tense Alexei had been banished. She had fallen asleep in the arms of a looser-limbed, becalmed man, and so he remained.

Kostya settled on the sand within the circumference of the umbrella and dug with a stick, making comments about the ant he was tracking. Alexei extended his hand and Maisy broke her rule, giving him hers. The peace and serenity of the moment settled very deeply over them.

It was, Maisy realised, sanctuary.

'I have to fly to Geneva on Friday,' he told her, his voice a register deeper, tugging on those muscles deep down inside her. It made her smile, and a response flared in his eyes. 'I want you to come with me.'

'I think Kostya and I should stay here,' she answered reluctantly. 'He's just starting to settle in. It would be wrong to disturb him.'

'Maria can look after him. It's only for a couple of days and a night.'

The night. He wanted her for the night. Maisy's toes curled with delight.

'A night too long.' She bit her lip, wishing it could be different. 'I can't leave him, Alexei.'

'No.' He looked out at the blue horizon, but Maisy knew he wasn't admiring the view. 'No,' he said again, his chest heaving in a deep sigh.

'You don't mind?' She wished she didn't sound so anxious. It made her sound needy and insecure.

'I mind, but I understand.' His thumb was running up and down over the palm of her hand. 'Leo didn't have parents for the first eight years of his life. It might explain why he didn't have as much time for his son as he probably should have. I won't make that mistake.'

Maisy stared at him. She hadn't known that, but Alexei's admission went a long way to healing the wound his words the other night had opened. So he *did* believe her—or was giving her the benefit of the doubt.

'But I travel a lot, Maisy. Kostya is going to have to get used to that.'

She tried to ignore the absence of herself in that statement. After all, what was between them wasn't for ever. But it was life for Kostya. 'Maybe in a few weeks, when he's secure?' she suggested.

'A week. He can have a week. Then I want you with me. I can't bring my life to a standstill, Maisy. It doesn't work that way.' He softened his tone. 'Besides, you'll go crazy here on your own. You need me to keep you entertained.'

'How entertaining will it be if you're working?'

'New York, Paris, Rome, Prague. Don't you want to see those cities?'

'I want to be with you,' said Maisy simply, because it was the truth.

He didn't answer her, but his hand remained secure around her own, and for all the tenuousness of her situation Maisy felt he would continue to hold her hand through this whole experience. She wouldn't think about it now—how it would be when he finally let her go.

CHAPTER NINE

'You smell so good.' They were in the apartment he kept in the fifth *arrondissement* of Paris. It had spectacular views, taking in the Seine and the spires of Notre Dame. It was the first time Maisy had been here and she was not a little overwhelmed by it all. She had expected sleek lines and into-the-future modernity from Alexei, but all around her was restrained Louis XVI cream-and-gold luxury.

It was like stepping into Paris in the eighteenth century. She loved it.

'I'm not wearing perfume.'

'Whatever.' He inhaled deeply as he nuzzled her neck.

Prickling all over in a good way, Maisy heard herself babbling, 'I just use this tangerine soap. That's probably what you smell…'

'I smell you, Maisy,' he growled in her ear, his big hands splaying over her waist as he dragged her in against him.

It was early morning and they had landed at Orly only an hour ago. Alexei had a long day ahead and they had both been up since 4:00 a.m. Admittedly she had slept on the plane and in the limo. Now she was wide-awake, her body starting to climb as his need for her made itself known.

'You smell good to me too,' she admitted, turning in his arms.

'Aftershave and soap,' he countered. 'Nothing fancy.'

But everything about him was fancy, thought Maisy, feeling utterly adored in his arms. He screamed wealth and good taste and leashed power—except when he was with her, in bed, and that was when she had him on her level. It was a strange alchemy of him being stripped to the essential bone, of him just being a male—albeit a very fine specimen—and her losing all of her everyday 'Maisyness' and becoming his equal, the woman he wanted.

The curves she despaired of back in London were all he wanted in his bed. Nothing she said or did with him in bed was ever wrong. His praise and response to her had given her such new-found confidence. Yet the rest of the time she didn't feel quite right.

They were constantly moving from Naples to Rome to Moscow to Madrid. She was always in limos, by herself or with Kostya, entering empty suites or apartments he kept in so many cities. Alexei sent stylists and personal shoppers to prepare her for dinner, usually in out-of-the-way places. He certainly didn't flaunt their relationship. Some evenings she ate alone. He claimed she would be bored at business dinners, and she was too unsure of her position to press the point. She now had clothing and jewellery brought to her by strangers to be worn for his pleasure. None of it was hers. She was always very careful. They didn't belong to her. She didn't want to damage them. She didn't know how to ask Alexei in the cold light of day what she should do with them.

So on this, her day in Paris, with Alexei tied up in talks and Kostya booked in with the children of friends of the Kulikovs, who were overjoyed to see him again, she hit the pavement in comfy flats and went shopping for herself.

She was footsore and faintly depressed on her return at seven. The personal shoppers had made it seem so easy, but the experience of trying on endless pieces that either didn't fit or made her feel dumpy or wrongly shaped or both hadn't been quite the fun she had anticipated.

Alexei was disconcerted that he had arrived home early, intending to surprise her, and learned she had gone out. He regarded the shopping bags on the bed as if they were alien.

She dragged out a pair of jeans and some comfy T-shirts, putting them in a neat pile, then produced the lovely fuchsia silk dress that had been the stellar purchase of her day, holding it up to show him.

'The shows are on next week, *dushka*,' he asserted dismissively. 'I will take you.'

Maisy hung on to her silk dress. *That* was his comment?

'I can't afford couture,' she said in an undertone.

He frowned.

'I mean, I know you want me to dress that way, and I appreciate it. But I wanted to get some clothes for myself today. It's a bit weird, always wearing borrowed clothes.'

'Maisy, the clothes belong to *you*. I got them for *you*. The clothes, the jewellery—whatever. It's yours.'

Maisy sat down on the bed, holding on to her dress. 'Oh.'

'Most women would be pleased,' he said.

It was the 'most women' that did it. Maisy smoothed out her new dress. 'Is that how it worked in the past? You dressed the women you were with?'

It was the first time she had raised the subject since the villa at Ravello, and Maisy experienced a wave of vertigo at the immensity of what lay underneath her question.

'No…' Alexei spoke slowly.

'Tara Mills, Frances Fielding, Kate Bernier.' She rattled off the names as if she were reading them from the tag on the back of her dress, because that was where her eyes were. She couldn't look at him. 'I don't suppose any of *them* needed help dressing up.'

'How in the hell did you get those names?'

The tightly leashed aggression in his voice brought her chin up. She wasn't backing down now. She had a right to know where she stood. He shouldn't be so defensive in telling her.

'I read about them in magazines,' she answered truthfully. 'It's okay, Alexei, everyone has a past. I'm not going to go postal.'

'I don't appreciate you researching me, Maisy. If you want

to know about my life, you only have to ask me.' He spoke in a perfectly reasonable tone, but his eyes were as cold as flints of ice.

She had crossed a line, Maisy realised with a sharp twinge of reaction. These were the limits to their relationship. She dressed for him, waited for him, slept with him, but she didn't ask him personal questions. Whatever he said.

'I seem to remember you had an investigation done into me,' she replied jerkily.

'Yes, because you were looking after my godson.'

Maisy squeezed the silk under her fingers as she made fists in her lap. 'And I read up about you because I am having sex with you every night.' And morning, and sometimes in the afternoon…

'I would rather you didn't look for information about me in the tabloids.'

'Fair enough,' she conceded. 'So, if you didn't dress them, why do you dress me?'

'I imagined it would make things easier for you.'

Yeah, right. This was about him being ashamed of her. 'I think I need to buy my own clothes,' she said, her voice amazingly calm given how shaken she was feeling. 'Buying me a wardrobe isn't a gift. It's…impersonal.'

'Impersonal?' He sounded as if he was trying out the word.

Maisy took a step into the abyss. 'It's kind of like you're buying me.'

Then he said absolutely the wrong thing. 'I've never paid for sex in my life.'

The aggression coming off him kept Maisy seated. 'I—I was talking about our relationship,' she faltered. All the while another voice was saying, *What relationship, Maisy? It's sex. He's always said it's sex. He just said it's sex.*

'I live a semi-public life.' He paced out, as tense as she had ever seen him. 'You need to be dressed for it if you're going to be with me.'

If. *If you're going to be with me.* Maisy's eyes were

starfish-wide as she cottoned on to what he was saying. Struggling to catch up, she recognised it for what it was. An ultimatum.

'You can't wear that—' he made a dismissive gesture at the pink silk puddled in her lap '—whatever it is. To dinner tonight.'

She hadn't been planning to. It was a dress for the daytime. But after all he'd said she was starting to feel completely surplus to his needs—had been feeling that way since they'd started travelling. And it was making her both terrified and very, very angry.

'There's nothing wrong with this dress,' she stated between her teeth.

'I want you in the champagne silk you wore in Rome.'

'No.'

'Fine.'

He turned away from her, removing his watch, his cufflinks. She watched him tumble them onto the bedside table. He headed for the walk-in wardrobe.

'Where are you going?'

He didn't answer, but a minute later he reappeared, naked. 'Shower,' he said briefly.

'I'm going to wear what I want to wear,' she defended herself. Why didn't he say anything?

'Do what you want,' he replied. 'The invitation is withdrawn.'

Maisy just gaped after him. What did he mean, the invitation was withdrawn? They weren't going to dinner? She couldn't believe what had just happened. Was he angry with her because she had bought her own clothes and refused his?

She heard the shower go on. Fine. She stood up too quickly and the room shifted slightly, so she sat down again. It had been such a long day—but, damn him, she wasn't going to be a pushover. Giving herself a few minutes to calm down, she fetched her brush and toiletries and marched into the bathroom. He was towelling himself dry and seemed a bit thrown to see her. But Maisy ignored him, shaking her hair out of its pins and pulling the brush through it with rough strokes.

'I'd like some space, Maisy.'

'Tough,' she replied, grabbing her spray conditioner and letting fly.

He wrapped the towel around his hips and left her to it. Maisy pushed down the pain and kept going, taming her curls into a neat chignon and then making up her eyes and mouth. When she emerged into the bedroom Alexei was dressed in trousers and was buttoning up a tailored white shirt. It clung faithfully to the wide expanse of his shoulders and chest like a sleeve, making him seem both overwhelmingly male and yet elegant at the same time. He was going out, she registered. Without her.

'Where are you going?'

When he didn't answer she hurled the brush she had in her hand at him, aiming for his legs and missing entirely. Her brush bounced on the luxurious carpet. He merely gave her a quelling look as if to say, *That's the best you can do?*

Not quite knowing what she was doing, but powered by the unfairness of it all, Maisy stripped off the simple shift she had been wearing all day, unhooked her plain cotton bra, slid off her knickers.

She kept her back to him. She had never undressed in front of him in all these weeks. There was something unfailingly intimate about it. Once she was in bed with him it was different. But the act of actually going about her daily robing and disrobing made her feel vulnerable, and she didn't need more of that.

She emptied out the bag of frothy nothings she had bought to wear for him, picking up a sheer black bra and knickers that had cost more than her pretty dress. The knickers had little bows at the side to be tied, and the bra had a bow at the front. Neither was at all practical for wearing anywhere other than in a bedroom to seduce a man.

Which had been her intention when she'd purchased them. Right now she had no idea *what* her intention was.

She adjusted her breasts into the cups, making sure they were secure, then cast a look at Alexei over her shoulder. He had got no further with his buttons from the moment she'd started stripping.

'Come and help me,' she requested, sounding petulant.

He didn't hesitate, which fired her confidence, and when he was only a hand-span away from her she turned around and untied the bow, so that the weight of her breasts tugged the bra cups apart.

'Do me up,' she instructed.

His hands moved obediently to slide under the fabric, his thumbs circling her nipples so that her head fell forward onto his chest. 'That's not helping me,' she murmured.

His voice was gratifyingly a register lower. 'You started this. I'll finish it.'

A lick of lust moved over her and she grabbed hold of his waistband, her hands trembling so that she was woeful at disengaging the buttons. But it didn't matter. He lifted her and she wrapped her bare legs around his hips. Ignoring the bed, he propelled her back against the wall, yanking the bows on her knickers free, testing her readiness with his fingers, lifting her again to slide his erection into her, his back and shoulders bunching up under her hands as he took the strain of doing it slowly and steadily and completely.

Maisy's head flopped forward, her hair cloaking them both as he buried his face in her neck and began to thrust into her with little finesse but a great deal of energy. Maisy couldn't stop the noises that were answering his rather effective grunts as she lost herself in the flashing pleasure.

That it could be like this startled her. That he could do this to her was almost overwhelming. No condom, she thought presently, straining against him. It must have hit him at the same time, because he seemed about to pull away from her, but his body continued to thunder forward and won out. Yet as he slid her down the wall and her feet touched carpet he pulled free and came over her bare stomach, holding himself with such an expression that Maisy never thought she had ever seen anything so beautiful. She felt like a goddess, all of her anger spent, all of him on her.

He was apologising to her, leaning against her, his head heavy, bent low, his breathing laboured, those big shoulders heaving. Maisy loved this. Loved the way she could do this to him. It made everything that had gone before somehow meaningless, as if this thing they shared overwhelmed the prosaic realities of the life they were living together.

Alexei was still in his shirt. He had stepped out of his boxers and trousers and Maisy had pushed the shirt back over his shoulders as they'd grappled. It hung suspended halfway down his back.

'You didn't come,' he muttered in her ear.

'Doesn't matter.' She wound her arms around him, burrowing, needing that closeness.

'You can wear what you want to dinner. We'll eat here. Whatever you want.'

Maisy hung on to him, but she had gone very still and quiet inside. Her instincts were telling her something and she didn't want to hear it right now. Easier just to take him at his word. But those words settled like stones in her belly.

This was her power over him. This was what she used for leverage. She had just manipulated a situation her way with sex. Those games he had tried to play with her early on and quickly given up she had now instigated as her own, however unconsciously.

But something about this relationship—probably to do with how it had started, the imbalances between them and Alexei's history—was changing her. Changing them.

She didn't want to be this woman. She didn't want to be this way with Alexei. She wanted honest, and real, and for him to love her. The realisation flashed with neon clarity across her mind. She was in love with him.

She wanted him to love her as she loved him. Had loved him from the moment she tore the lining of his jacket and he had looked at her, really looked at her, and she had seen him and recognised in him something she needed very much.

And right now all the danger signs were flashing red.

The first night they were back in Ravello Alexei dreamt of St Petersburg.

He was eight years old and on the streets. He ran in a pack of kids, all of them living hand-to-mouth. He couldn't remember his father, but he could still see his mother's stunning face, cosmetically enhanced, bending in and blowing alcohol into his lungs. Promising she would return for him in a few days but never coming back.

He woke bathed in sweat, shaking. Blackness was all around him and he was alone.

Maisy woke to the sound of a shout. She sat up, no longer disorientated when she woke in the night to find herself in a vast bed. Falling asleep every night pinned by Alexei's arm had made what was once so novel an integral part of her everyday life.

Alexei was awake. It was too dark to see his face, but she could feel the startled reaction running through his big warm body. He'd had another one of those dreams. She reached out in the darkness and laid her hand on his chest. It was hot and hair-roughened and rose fast under her hand.

'Are you okay?' she whispered.

He rolled away, dislodging her hand and presenting the bulk of his back and shoulders to her.

Maisy was wide-awake now. She didn't know what to do. The other time he'd woken in the night like this he had pretended to go back to sleep, but they both knew he had lain awake most of the night.

'Alexei,' she whispered, 'talk to me.'

He made that grunting noise she recognized, which told her she could wrap her arms around him but not expect much communication. So she did, lying down and wrapping her arms around his middle. Alexei sought her hands, knotting them with his and lashing her against him.

He could feel her breath against his back, the soft brush of her wayward hair, the sweet rub of her smooth calf over his. It soothed.

He said, half to himself, 'Kostya will be all right.'

His voice was hoarse and Maisy was instantly on high alert. Something was very wrong.

'Of course he will be.' She spoke feelingly but she felt uncertain. A couple of weeks had passed now since Kostya had been told of his parents' deaths. Alexei had been amazing with him, giving both her and Kostya the strong bulwark they both needed in those awful fragile days as the tiny child groped for security.

Maisy had broken her rule on those nights, having Kostya in bed with her to soothe his night terrors. Alexei had volunteered to take the other bed but Kostya had wanted his beloved Alessi too, and what Maisy had most feared had come to pass. They were a facsimile of a family, huddled together in this vast bed that had once seemed so alien and threatening but was now where all the happiest times of her life were spent.

'I'll protect him,' Alexei asserted.

'I know.' She stroked his back.

He tried to clutch on to the human warmth of her touch, but he was being swamped by his own fears from the past and they were fast dragging him under. It coalesced the longer he lay there, beginning to tense under the feel of her touch. He had allowed her to get too close and he knew the terror he was feeling was a warning. She too would leave. It was inevitable one of them would abandon what they had. He had to reinstate proper distance. He could not allow his own fear or weakness to dislodge the grip he had on his emotions. He had to do it now.

Abruptly he shifted, dislodging Maisy's hold, and reached up, flicking on the lamp.

'I can't protect him from you, can I?'

He watched her blinking blearily in the unexpected light, covering her eyes with her hands. Defenceless. But he needed to be brutal. She needed to hear this.

'What are you talking about, Alexei?'

'I'm talking about you leaving, Maisy. Because we both know there's an end date.'

She stared back at him, appalled. A slow cold trickle of dread made its way down her spine.

'Why are you attacking me?' she whispered. 'It's the middle of the night.'

Then he said the words she had been dreading in the darkest part of her soul. 'I can't do this any more, Maisy.'

A tiny, endlessly hopeful, naive part of her had imagined a future with him—one involving a white dress, a picket fence and babies. The things she'd longed for when she was a little girl and the world had been a much more black-and-white place. But she knew now that wasn't going to happen. Not with this man.

Weeks of living with him, sleeping beside him, welcoming him into her body, and she understood she hadn't really touched anything beyond his surface. These dreams she sensed were a gateway into whatever darkness was eating away at him, but even lying in bed with him, privy to their ragged effect on him, she was not invited inside.

'I see.' It was all she could think to say, although she didn't see at all. But it was three o'clock in the morning and he was ripping her heart out and she hadn't even seen it coming.

Although in retrospect the signs had all been there. Despite the travel, they had essentially been alone. She hadn't minded a bit, because she'd had Alexei and Kostya, but it said volumes for where he saw her in his life. She remembered those photographs in the magazines, those women on his arm. That would never be her. He had never intended that to be her. She was like some sort of secret he kept.

Deep down she'd known this day was going to come. But it

made no sense—not at three o'clock, not just hours after she'd fallen asleep in his arms, her body still bearing the traces of his lovemaking. He couldn't be tired of her yet. He was just shucking off the effects of his nightmare. If she stayed very still and very small he might just go back to sleep and forget about it. But she wasn't that girl any more. She had changed. She had grown up.

She watched a deep breath shudder through him, and he said almost hopelessly, 'Are you happy with me, Maisy?'

'Yes.' *I've never been so happy. I've never felt so right in my whole life.*

'You never go anywhere. You never see anyone.' He propped himself up against the headboard.

'I see you,' she said. 'I see Kostya.'

He was trying to persuade her to leave.

'We can't keep this up. It's starting to get on my nerves.' He looked down at her. 'We need to be with other people, out in the world, or this is never going to be normal.'

What on earth was he talking about? Maisy wanted to shake him, but she sensed half of this was about his pain and the strange hour and the stillness. If she kept quiet he might just say something revealing, something that would let her in just a fraction.

But she couldn't help murmuring, 'You want to see other people?'

'Maybe you need a job,' he said instead. 'You need a life of your own.'

It hurt. 'I have a job. I look after Kostya. I have a life.'

'For how long?' He turned his head and she was shocked by the tension bracketed around his mouth and eyes. He looked older, tired.

'I think that rather depends on you.' There—she'd said it.

'If I had my way we'd never leave this bed.'

But his expression didn't soften and he was done talking. She knew there would be no revelations tonight. She knew she should push, but his words were pounding in her head: *we can't keep this up; we need to be with other people; you need a life of your own.* And it all contained the same message: *you're not enough any more.*

'Can we go to sleep?' She voiced the last thing she wanted to do.

He stretched across and the light went out. Maisy waited for him to reach for her, but he didn't. He remained upright, sitting still and silent in the dark.

Rolling over, making herself as small and unobtrusive as possible, she stared into a bleak future without him and she too didn't sleep.

'There's a boatload of people turning up at noon. I thought I'd put them on the yacht instead of dragging them through here, but there's a small group who will be staying overnight. Do you think you can handle that?'

Alexei delivered this with the unconcern of a man who issued orders on a daily basis. It was just he had never issued an order to *her*, and Maisy didn't quite know how to react.

He looked amazing this morning, in an olive-green polo shirt and tailored chinos, freshly shaven and no doubt smelling of tangy aftershave and male skin, but Maisy didn't know because he hadn't so much as bussed her cheek since their early-morning discussion.

Now he was springing this on her. People were coming? He hadn't said a word.

'I'm usually quite good with people,' she ventured. They were eating breakfast in the dining room. Maisy never felt entirely comfortable, perched at the end of the long table. Alexei's place was set beside hers, but he had managed to set his chair back and Maisy didn't feel their usual morning connection, when he sat so close she could hook her foot around his ankle and rub up his calf. She wasn't rubbing anything this morning.

'I know. I've seen you in action. The staff love you.' He sipped his espresso as if it held his attention. But Maisy wasn't fooled. His highwire brain was on the job. 'However, after today it'll be official. People will want to know who you are.' He turned his head slowly, fixed her with those blue eyes. 'What do I tell them?'

I'm your girlfriend, Maisy wanted to scream at him. *I love you. I've loved you for every minute of every hour of every day since I laid eyes on those handmade Italian shoes. You're everything to me. You bring the day and you hang the moon, you stupid idiot.*

'Tell them I'm Maisy Edmonds and I look after Kostya,' she said, kicking back her chair, feeling furious with him and sick to death of herself. 'And that when I'm done supervising his meals and making sure he gets enough sleep, I look after you.'

She made to stalk off, and it would have been a great exit, but he reached out and leashed her wrist, dragging her onto his lap. She sat stiff and affronted, refusing to look at him.

'I'll send a car for you at one. Carlo will come with you on the launch.'

'I *hate* Carlo,' she said with a passion, not sure why she'd chosen now to tell him.

'What has he done?' Alexei's gaze sharpened on her.

'He's a pig. He thinks you've bought me. Ever since you gave me those stupid cards and that smart phone.'

'I've never seen you use it once.'

'I put it in a drawer. I don't need it,' she dismissed, annoyed they were talking about gadgets instead of what mattered: her and him, and where they stood. 'I don't need any of it.'

'The money is there for you to spend, *dushka*. I want you to enjoy yourself.'

Maisy sighed heavily. He was never going to understand how she felt. 'I've told you, Alexei, I don't want your stupid money.'

He'd given her a bank account, but he'd never so much as given her a bunch of flowers. Everything was rising to the surface today, and now she had to face a host of strangers, and be introduced as what? Alexei's latest accessory?

'Can you be ready at one?'

'Do I have a choice?'

He stroked the curve of her jaw, encouraging her to look at him.

'I think I told you once before, *dushka*, you always have choices. You made one when you decided to be with me, and now I need you to abide by your choice a little longer.' He dislodged her from his lap. 'Off you go. And I've organised a little help for your dress.'

Maisy puzzled over this enigmatic statement until midmorning, when a stylist arrived at the house. She was sorting out Kostya's washing when Maria let her know over the intercom, and she came down in jeans and a stained T-shirt, her hair pulled back in an elastic band.

The woman had clearly been paid a good deal of money, because she barely raised a perfectly groomed eyebrow, but Maisy was whisked upstairs immediately. Apparently two hours was going to be pushing it to get her ready.

It was gruelling. She was plucked, waxed, polished, made up, brushed, stripped, and dipped into a hot pink silk and chiffon dress that fell from spaghetti straps from her shoulders, skimmed her breasts and flounced over her knees. She stepped into silver sandals. Her hair was elaborately plaited and pinned, tendrils artfully brimming around her made-up face. Her eyes looked like mysterious pools with all the kohl, and her mouth was as fresh as a pink rose.

Maisy could categorically say she had never felt beautiful in her life.

And she felt beautiful now.

'Bellissima,' murmured the stylist's assistant.

Maisy blinked rapidly. Tears were going to ruin the effect of her eyes.

'I've never had a client cry before,' said the stylist, gently dabbing Maisy's lashes.

Except she wasn't emotional about the dress, the make-up,

the look; she was thinking that if Alexei saw her looking like
this he might keep her a little longer, that she might stand a
chance against his lifetime ingrained habit of treating women
like expensive toys.

She didn't want to end up like her smart phone. In a
drawer, out of sight, out of mind. Redundant to needs and circumstances.

Maisy stayed below deck to protect her hair from the wind
during the high speed trip in the motor launch to the floating
palace that was called *Firebird*.

It was her first visit to the yacht, although Alexei had pointed
it out to her with binoculars. He had casually commented he
used it mainly for entertaining, and as he hadn't been entertaining anyone but her there had been no need to go there.

Clearly her entertainment value was on the wane.

There was something about seeing the sleek lines of the
yacht and experiencing its vast size up close that had Maisy
once more thinking about what this opulence must do to someone's sense of self. Yet for all his wealth Alexei was remark-
ably down to earth. It was a big part of why she had fallen in
love with him.

The yacht was buzzing with activity. Another tender was
arriving as she stepped aboard, and Maisy felt an unexpected
flutter of nerves. She was naturally shy, but had worked very
hard to practise her social skills, so that she could usually make
friends wherever she went. But these people were Alexei's
friends, and that thought sent her over the edge. She needed to
pull herself together and remember there was no reason why
they wouldn't like her, that there was nothing out of the ordinary in her situation. In this world mistresses were an *expected*
addition to a successful man. And, although Alexei had never
used that word, Maisy now understood he believed it was the
only position in his life a woman could occupy.

As she was escorted into the main salon she saw people on
the foredeck actively craning their necks to get a glimpse of

her. It was an odd sensation, and Maisy wasn't sure she liked it. The attendant with her knocked briefly on a door, then nodded to Maisy and retreated.

'Enter.'

Maisy felt very odd, waiting for permission to enter Alexei's presence. He was applying cufflinks to his suit and he dropped one of them as he looked up and fastened his eyes on her.

She went to pick it up but he caught her hand, raising her up. 'I want to look at you.'

His approval should have been gratifying, but Maisy was finding it difficult to enjoy it.

'You look so different,' he said, his accent thicker than usual.

'It's the hair and the make-up,' she dismissed, trying to make light of it. 'It's still me underneath the scaffolding.' She tried not to seem too eager, but couldn't help asking, 'Are you going to kiss me?'

'Of course.' He brushed his lips over her cheek.

Disappointed, Maisy tried to justify his coolness. She was wearing lipstick; they were both dressed up; he probably didn't want to reek of her perfume...

'You look beautiful,' she said impulsively, touching his jacket, straightening what was already straight.

'That's my line,' he replied, subtly drawing away.

But it hadn't been his line. *Different* had been his line.

'I'm nervous,' she blurted out.

'Don't be. They're only people.'

'They're your friends.'

'No, Maisy, for the most part they're just a crowd. You'll enjoy yourself. I'd ask you to keep a lid on the Kostya situation, if you would. People are curious, but it's none of their business.'

The Kostya situation? 'I don't quite understand.'

Alexei scooped up the gold cufflink. 'Simple. I'll be blunt. Don't tell people you're the nanny.'

He gave her a brief taut smile, as if trying to take the edge off his words.

'No,' Maisy said quietly, 'I wouldn't do that. It would be humiliating for me, considering my circumstances now.'

'We're not going to have an argument right now, are we, *dushka*?' He was smiling but his eyes were hard. 'So close to showtime?'

'No, no argument.' She focussed on his hands, fumbling with his cuff, and instinctively reached out and took the cuff-link from him, fastening it to his sleeve in silence. She could feel him breathing so close to her. She stroked his wrist with her fingertips and his breathing hitched. It was the reassurance she needed. She lifted his hand and pressed her lips to his palm. It was then she realised why he had been having so much trouble with the cufflink. His hands were shaking.

Yesterday she would have asked him why. Today she gave him her best smile. 'No one will notice lipstick on your hand, and if they do—' her smile faltered only a little '—you can tell them it's just a token of affection from your mistress.'

He didn't correct her.

CHAPTER TEN

MAISY had felt overdressed as she was sped towards the yacht. Now, amidst so much luxury and Alexei's guests, she was glad of her clothes and hair and insubstantial sandals. Some of these women were utterly breathtaking. The men were all cool and sharp and controlled. She recognised the type. She had been living with a prince of the blood for several weeks.

She desperately wanted to cling on to Alexei's hand when she came out into the sunshine on his arm, but she knew deep down any sign of vulnerability would bring her closer to the edge of their relationship. She really didn't want to fall today. Not in front of all these people.

Yet her fragility threatened to undermine her with every step. The heels on her sandals clicked on the teak decking, the silken underskirt of her dress flowed over her hips and thighs like cool water, yet her skin felt hot and tight and her throat ached from everything she was holding inside her.

Alexei had completely metamorphosed into a cool stranger and she was out of her depth. They were back to where they had been at midnight on that strange night weeks ago in London. It was as if all that had happened between them had been a feverish dream and at any moment he was going to look down at her and demand to know who in the hell she was.

It shocked her when he suddenly sped up, let go of her hand, and crashed into a bear hug with another man. It was genuine. As was his greeting to another equally imposing man. The women with them flashed smiles and a lot of jewellery, and kissed him joyfully in the European fashion.

Maisy tried not to gape. They all spoke in Russian at once, and as the seconds ticked by she felt more and more excluded, although they were all darting looks at her, waiting for Alexei to introduce her. If she had felt more confident she would have enjoyed his clear enthusiasm in the moment, but instead it only underlined how differently he was treating her.

'Hello,' she said abruptly to the woman standing closest to her. 'I'm Maisy.'

'Stefania,' said the girl, beaming at her, then darting a look at Alexei.

'Maisy, this is Valery and Ivanka Abramov, and Stiva and Stefania Lieven. Maisy Edmonds.'

'Alexei has told us absolutely nothing about you,' said Stiva, giving Alexei a curious look.

'Well, I'm sure we can get to know her now,' interposed the brunette Ivanka.

She gave Maisy a wink, and instantly some of the tension in Maisy's shoulders eased.

'Your dress is gorgeous,' Stefania joined in. 'Who designed it?'

'I don't know,' Maisy said, darting a nervous look towards Alexei. 'Sorry.'

She could have kicked herself. She sounded like a complete moron. But the other girls were chattering on about designers, and the two men, although speaking to Alexei, kept glancing her way with reassuring smiles, helping her feel welcomed to their inner circle.

She appreciated their effort, but everything about these two couples screamed 'married' and it only made her feel more isolated. Not to mention the fact Stefania kept being roped back into Stiva's arms, giggling and blushing. Anyone with eyes in their head could see they were in love. And, whilst Ivanka was more circumspect, there was an easy quality between her and Valery. All she and Alexei had was this wall, and she couldn't see over it, had no idea how to begin scaling it, and doubted it was ever going to come down.

After half an hour Ivanka drifted away to make a phone call regarding her children and Alexei moved Maisy on, although she could see he was reluctant. These were clearly his friends, and the people he had spoken of who would be staying at the house. The rest were the crowd. Yet he made his way dutifully through them and Maisy trailed him. Whenever he smiled at her or touched her it was for public consumption.

He detached himself from her after several introductions, making sure she had a glass of mineral water in her hand, brushing her fingertips with his lips—once more for show, she realised sadly. Fortunately she managed to drift and be drawn into one group or another. Everyone wanted to speak to her. Was she enjoying the Amalfi Coast? Alexei had gone un-usually AWOL, and now everyone knew why. And who could blame him? This was a theme with few variations. It embar-rassed her and she didn't know what to say. She was offered champagne and took it. As she was propelled from one knot of people to another there was always another glass.

Then at last she was sitting down by herself, protected from the hot sun by an awning. She felt fuzzy from the champagne she had consumed for Dutch courage. Was it three glasses? Four? She'd lost count. Her glass had never seemed to be empty and she'd just kept sipping. Her shoes pinched and her face hurt from smiling.

'You must be Maisy.' A tall, slender woman in an almost transparent white shift was standing over her. Her black hair fell in a faultless waterfall to her shoulders. She was vaguely familiar. 'We haven't been introduced. Tara Mills.'

Maisy accepted the hand that was offered.

'We have Alexei in common,' she said, sitting down, cross-ing impossibly long and elegant tanned bare legs. Maisy drew her pale ones in under her. 'You don't mind, do you?'

Perhaps another woman would have thrown the contents

of her drink in Tara's perfect face, but Maisy was feeling distinctly generous. So this was the former mistress.

'I need another drink,' she replied instead, looking around.

Tara merely lifted a hand and a waiter arrived with a tray of them. In any other circumstances it would have been funny. Tara and Alexei were perfectly matched. A snap of her fingers and the world came to a halt and then turned on its axis for Tara Mills.

Tara held out her glass and clinked Maisy's. 'To our mutual friend.'

'He may be your friend but he's not mine,' she said without thinking.

'Trouble in paradise?' Tara placed a slender hand on Maisy's bare knee, drawing Maisy's attention to its round curve in comparison to Tara's bony leg.

'No.' Maisy felt driven to deny it and took a deep swallow. The alcohol buzzed through her system and she knew without a doubt the day was going to end badly.

'You're to do with the Kulikov baby, aren't you?' Tara set down her untouched glass. 'He was obsessed with rescuing the little thing.'

'Rescuing?' Maisy echoed, letting down her guard.

'Oh, you know what they're like, the hyped-up brotherhood. As soon as news of Leo's accident came in they were all lining up to adopt the boy. Alexei won. Alexei always wins, doesn't he?'

Maisy tried to process this jigsaw of information. Alexei was Kostya's godfather, but what on earth was the brotherhood?

'What I'm *dying* to know—and you're going to tell me, Maisy—is where you come into the picture. A little bird tells me you were the *nanny*, but that can't be right. Alexei's got too much class to sleep with the nanny.'

'I don't know,' Maisy said fuzzily. 'He slept with you. His standards must be pretty low.'

Tara didn't blink. 'Oh, Maisy, you're a funny little thing.

Make sure he puts your goodbye package into shares—they'll last longer.'

Suddenly Maisy was so very glad he had never given her any jewellery. All of that stuff she'd worn she considered on loan. Tara was wearing a single sapphire pendant that hung low between her small high breasts, but all Maisy could see was the diamonds she had seen in the magazine photograph. He had bought Tara. Just as he'd bought this luxury yacht.

He didn't buy me, she told herself. *That's the difference. He didn't buy me.*

Tara stood up. 'Just one more word of advice, Maisy. Today? He invited me.'

Maisy spilled her champagne. She stared blankly as the liquid soaked into her expensive lap, darkening into a wide stain.

'Oh, honey.' It was Ivanka, instantly at her side, putting the glass to one side, sliding a maternal arm around her waist. 'We need to fix you up. Can you walk?'

Maisy nodded, unable to speak because she needed all her concentration to keep herself together and take a step, and then another. She was grateful for Ivanka's sturdy arm around her waist and her knowledge of the yacht. When they reached one of the staterooms Ivanka led her straight to the bathroom.

'Take off the dress. We need to soak the stain.'

As Maisy hesitated Ivanka grinned at her. 'You really are a sweetheart. I'll fetch you a robe.'

Stripped, Maisy waited in her knickers, arms crossed over her bare breasts. She ventured out into the stateroom, feeling distinctly woozy. For a moment she couldn't move because a man was standing in the doorway. He said something in a foreign language and Maisy made a sound, stumbling back into the bathroom and slamming shut the door. She leaned against it, terrified of what was going on. She didn't know how long she waited, heart pounding, before there was a brief knock on the door.

'Maisy, it's Ivanka.'

Maisy slid away from the door. She wrapped the robe around

herself gratefully. 'There was a man in the doorway,' she said shakily. 'He saw me.'

Ivanka swore quietly. She squeezed Maisy's hand. 'You're okay?'

'I think I'm drunk.'

'Yeah, I saw Baba Yaga casting her evil spell. Don't believe anything she told you, Maisy. She's had a hard time adjusting to life post-Ranaevsky.'

I can imagine, thought Maisy drearily. She was feeling distinctly light-headed. The room was beginning to spin.

'I think I need to lie down,' she revealed shakily.

'Right.'

Ivanka got her to the bed, and the moment Maisy's head touched the pillow the whole room started to lurch. She groaned. 'Don't leave me,' she pleaded.

'I've got your back, honey.' The mattress sank a little as Ivanka perched beside her. 'You don't drink, I take it?'

'No.'

'Well, Tara Mills would drive anyone to it. You know…' She stroked Maisy's temple. 'I think he picks them because they're the last women in the world who'll get under his skin. Which makes you a freaking miracle.'

Maisy suddenly wished she was a million miles from drunk. This woman knew the secrets of the universe, and this was her chance to make sense of them.

Ivanka smiled at her, as if sensing her unspoken need to know. 'My husband Valery—you met him earlier,' she prompted. 'He and Alexei go right back to the orphanage.'

Orphanage? Maisy's eyes snapped open. 'Is this something to do with the brotherhood?'

'Brotherhood? Oh, Tara strikes again. There is no brotherhood. It's just the four boys—well, three now that Leo's gone.' Ivanka crossed herself reflexively.

Maisy's tired brain did some quick turns. Orphanage in Russia. Four boys. Suddenly Alexei's life opened up before her and darkness rushed in. The dreams. Last night. The way he was behaving today. Maybe it wasn't about her. She thought she was the centre of his life because he was hers. But it wasn't about her.

An orphanage?

He never talked about his family and she had never asked, afraid he would ask about hers. Now she wished she had—wished she had shown more courage.

'I didn't know,' she said heavily.

Ivanka smiled, looking at her curiously. 'He hasn't told you? I'm not surprised. I didn't get the entire story for a year—a full year, might I add—into my marriage. It took me a difficult pregnancy to get it out of Valery. And Alexei's a whole different kettle of fish. Need-to-know basis.'

'I need to know.' Maisy tried to sit up, but Ivanka laid a gentle hand on her shoulder.

'Lie still. You'll only feel worse. Here's the deal. The boys met up in an orphanage as kids. You can't know what Russian orphanages are like, Maisy. It's not like here or in England. It's pretty primitive. The story goes Alexei broke them out and the boys lived independently on the city streets, sleeping in parks, cemeteries, anywhere they could. Basements of public buildings in the long winters.'

Maisy did sit up now. 'But what about the authorities? Wasn't anything done?'

'No one cared, Maisy. Homeless children are everywhere in my country. Valery says if it wasn't for Alexei they'd all be dead. He had that "survival of the fittest" instinct even at eight.'

'Eight?' Maisy framed the word, not quite believing it. 'And no parents?'

'Oh, Alexei had parents. I think that's what made him as tough as he is. His father took off when he was very young, and his mother just came home one day and told him she was going on a little break for a few days and would be back for him. She never came.'

'What happened to her?' Maisy asked, aware she wasn't going to like the answer.

'Who knows? Probably a new man, a better opportunity. She'd have been finding it hard to ply her trade with a seven-year-old boy around her neck.'

'Her trade?'

'She was a prostitute.'

Maisy suddenly really didn't want to be having this conversation with Ivanka. She didn't know her. She knew Alexei would consider what she was doing a betrayal, but what choice did she have if he wouldn't talk to her about any of this?

His mother had abandoned him. A seven-year-old. Instantly a much younger Alexei flashed into her mind—a little boy with innocent blue eyes and long lashes and a frail child's body, trying to survive those Russian winters without anyone to protect him. It was that stark. And it suddenly made absolute sense that he would storm Lantern Square with a truckload of security. He was doing for Kostya what nobody had done for him.

'How did they survive?'

'Cunning, street smarts, not knowing anything else.' Ivanka gave a little shrug, but Maisy could see how much it affected the other woman to talk about it. 'Valery and Stiva ended up back in an institution, but then Alexei and Leo got lucky. The Kulikovs took them in. They made Leo their son.'

'And Alexei?'

'They had other children. It was decided Alexei was too far gone. He'd be a bad influence.' Ivanka spoke matter-of-factly. 'He was running a cigarette scam for a local crime boss by the time he was eleven, Maisy. I don't blame Marfa Kulikov one bit. But she always opened up her home to the boys on holidays, gave them all a break from the relentlessness of their lives. Probably saved Alexei's life. I know for a fact he still lights a candle for her on her saint's day.'

Something hard and fast lodged in Maisy's chest.

'But Alexei's always been the smart one. He knew he'd end up getting swept into some serious violence if he didn't find something legit. That's when he got the boys organised with the boats. He started up a boat-hire business when he was fifteen on Lake Ladoga. It gave all four of them their start. None of them have done too badly.'

'I don't know what to say,' was all Maisy could murmur.

'Just don't tell Alexei I spilled. It would cause all sorts of problems between him and Valery. Leo's death has hit them all hard, but Alexei hardest. They were the closest, those two. I always got the impression Alexei looked after Leo, but Leo gave Aloyshia the emotional support he needed and didn't get elsewhere.'

Aloyshia. Maisy flinched at the casual affection in that name. Years. He had known these people for years. They were his blood and his bone, his family. These were the people he confided in.

He had told her nothing. But then, she hadn't asked.

'Now, before we both start crying, how is little Kostya? I'm dying to see him. Whenever we saw Anais and Leo he was never with them. I suspect he was at home with you.'

'Yes, I looked after Kostya for two years.' Maisy didn't see the point of evading the truth.

'Which is how you and Alexei met. You're very young to have been raising a child. I got the impression Anais didn't spend very much time at home.'

Maisy had no intention of defaming her friend, but Ivanka seemed to understand this and laid a warm hand on hers.

'Leo chose a highly strung racehorse and wondered why she didn't turn into a brood mare when he got her in the stable. They're Valery's words, not mine. I'm a brood mare, Maisy, and happy to be one. I've got two boys of my own—Nicky and Sasha—you'll meet them tonight. You, on the other hand, seem more like a filly to me, which makes it hard to imagine how you manage a two-year-old boy. Actually, I don't know how you manage the thirty-year-old one.'

'I don't. Not very well,' Maisy confessed. She was finding Ivanka very easy to talk to.

'Tell me how you and Alexei met.'

'He attacked me in the Kulikovs' kitchen.'

'Okay—so far, so not Alexei.' Ivanka laughed. 'Do tell, Maisy.'

So Maisy started at the beginning, picking her way through the rubble of the past few weeks, explaining about Anais and looking after Kostya, and the outrageous way Alexei had stormed into the house.

'That's Alexei—never does things by halves,' was all Ivanka said.

Maisy edited out herself in a towel, him throwing her up against the door, and moved on to coming to Ravello. 'And then I fell in love with him,' she said simply. It was the first time she had said it aloud, and the fact that it wasn't to Alexei, that it could never be to Alexei, opened the floodgates.

She cried. For herself, but mainly for the little boy who had been abandoned by his mother and left to fend for himself. Ivanka stroked her head throughout, until a strange sort of peace invaded Maisy's body. And with it the nausea rose. She just made it to the bathroom in time.

And that was where Alexei found her.

'She's drunk.'

Alexei sounded incredulous, and in the old days—the days before today—Maisy would have laughed. But she was too busy being gloriously ill into a mercifully pristine toilet bowl.

Ivanka said something in Russian. Something that silenced Alexei. And in the silence Maisy slid onto her bottom, shutting her eyes against the suddenly clear certainty that she had disgraced herself.

The problem with nausea was that now it had passed she felt a reprieve—enough to realise how appalling her situation was. She awkwardly got to her feet, flushing the toilet and refusing to look at Alexei as she struggled to the sink, filling a glass with cold water and rinsing out her mouth. The mirror wasn't kind: she looked white, her fancy hairstyle beginning to come apart. The robe gaped open and she sashed it tightly, her eyes going anxiously to his.

Alexei's whole body told the story of how angry he was with her. His arms just hung at his sides, and he was tense and frozen to the spot.

Ivanka was gone. Wise woman, thought Maisy, drawing her arms about her waist. She needed a hug, and Alexei wasn't going to provide it.

It was hard to feel sorry for him when he was towering over her, all two hundred pounds of Russian machismo, judging her.

'Are you all right?'

He was *very* angry, she recognized. His accent was so thick she had to concentrate to understand him.

She nodded. 'Ivanka helped me. She's very kind.'

Alexei said something under his breath.

'How much did you drink?'

'I don't know.'

'You don't drink.' He sounded almost helpless.

Maisy met his eyes in the mirror. 'I didn't do a lot of things until today,' she muttered, leaning into the sink.

'Where's your dress? Why are you undressed?' He framed the question roughly.

'I spilt champagne on it. Ivanka took it to soak.' She took a shuddery breath. 'I think a man was here and saw me. When I didn't have any clothes on.'

'I heard about it.' The last scrap of colour left Maisy's face. He made a European gesture with his hands. 'Don't look like that,' he said urgently. 'I've taken care of it.'

'What do you mean?' she whispered.

'Everyone's gone. I've emptied the boat.'

'Oh.' *Oh.*

Alexei shifted on his feet. He wasn't angry with her, Maisy registered. Something else was going on.

He had emptied the boat. Because of her. Was he taking care of her?

'Did he speak to you? Touch you?'

Maisy shook her head. 'I shut myself in here. I didn't leave the door open even a crack.'

His expression altered. He took a step towards her. *Why isn't he holding me*? her nerves were shrieking.

'I don't regret that,' he said in a driven undertone. 'I refuse to regret London, but I'm sorry if I made you feel manhandled.'

Manhandled? Maisy wrapped her arms around her waist again, knowing someone had to hold her. 'It didn't feel that way,' she answered honestly, wondering why they were back to talking about London again, and then another wave of nausea crashed over her and with a moan she zeroed in on the toilet bowl.

'Go away,' she got out, before she began retching on an empty stomach. She felt Alexei's hands on her shoulders, hovering. 'The glamour of being your mistress,' she mumbled, wiping her wet mouth with the back of her hand and not caring. She slumped on the floor, head and shoulders down. She didn't want to see anything like disgust on his face.

To her astonishment, Alexei hunkered down beside her, his face close to hers, his eyes haunted, his features stark in the pallor of his strained face. In a moment of blinding clarity Maisy realised he had looked this way all day, only it was worse now. He was *suffering*, and all she had done all day was worry about herself, her feelings, her misery.

And now she knew his.

'It's all right,' she said, smoothing her hand over his jaw instinctively. 'I'm here.'

But it wasn't the right thing to say. He flinched, then covered it by offering her his hand. When she didn't take it he scooped her up as if she were a little doll. Maisy didn't even bother to fight him. She was feeling all sorts of empty. He might as well carry her shell wherever he wanted to put it.

'You're not well. You need to lie down.' It was not an instruction or even a declaration. He was just speaking aloud. He wasn't having conversations with her any more. He hadn't been all day. His brief fracture in the bathroom had healed over. There was no sign he even cared about her any more.

'I want to get off this boat,' she said in a low voice. 'I want to go home.'

He laid her on the bed, speared a hand through his hair, looking out of the window at the smooth blue water. It was late afternoon—that lazy, warm time in early summer. He didn't even see it. He felt cold. He'd felt cold all day. Sixtieth-parallel-cold—the kind of chill you only got in a St Petersburg winter.

Seventeenth of May. He always spent this day on this boat, surrounded by people. Well, the people had gone, and there was only Maisy, looking so pale and wounded, and struggling with him over inanities. She didn't have a clue. He'd dragged her around all day but he hadn't actually absorbed anything she had said or done or asked of him.

But he wasn't going to forget how he'd felt when one of his male guests, the son of shipping magnate Aristotle Kouris, had made the mistake of telling Stiva that 'Ranaevsky's mistress' was cavorting naked in one of the staterooms. The fear had torn through him. If Valery hadn't been there he would have killed Kouris. But first he'd had to get to Maisy. Valery had called a halt to proceedings and he had bulleted down here, to find Maisy in bed all right, but not being attacked, being comforted by Ivanka, who had given him an old-fashioned look he didn't want to analyse right now.

And she was drunk and sick and vulnerable. And ashamed. He felt her shame like a palpable thing. It was about all that he *was* feeling.

He had to tell her, he realised. He had to say something. At least it might give both of them a reprieve.

'Maisy, I'm a bit toxic at the moment. You need to give me a wide berth. Can you do that?'

She had dragged her legs off the bed, the robe had come open, and she was struggling to make herself decent. In a far off part of his brain the rueful thought occurred that despite everything she was still shy about her body, still modest… And without warning it all played out in his head. London. He had been thinking about it all afternoon.

London.

She had never invited him in. He had invaded her privacy, overridden her modesty and *taken* her. Snatched and grabbed and *manhandled* her. Just like every man who had come trudging through that one-room apartment, hitched up his mother's dress and done his business. Then left money on the kitchen table. Money for her drink and her clothes and her drug habit. If it hadn't been for the neighbours he would have starved.

Maisy moistened her dry lips. 'For how long do you want me to keep away from you?'

'Just today. Give me the rest of today.' His voice was deep and black and lost.

She bent her head. There was nothing more to say.

Except an image of a small boy with brilliant blue eyes seared her mind's eye and she lifted her head.

'No,' she said.

Maisy stood up, her eyes never leaving his.

'No,' she repeated.

He actually looked panicked. Cool, oh-so-sure-of-himself Alexei Ranaevsky looked panicked. She stepped towards him and he backed up as if she was armed and dangerous. Maisy stopped.

'Ivanka told me about the orphanage.'

Something flickered behind those magnetic eyes, then closed down and Maisy found herself looking into obsidian. She swallowed, watching Alexei's familiar features harden with every passing second, his cheekbones more pronounced, his Tartar heritage never more obvious as his eyes narrowed on her.

'Ivanka had no business doing that.' His voice was hard.

'Maybe not, but you'd never have told me. Alexei, you were seven years old!'

He didn't even flinch.

She couldn't bear the bleakness in his eyes.

'What's the significance of today?'

He continued to look through her and Maisy felt her resolve slipping. But she had to try. Knowing even as she closed the distance between them and slid her arms around his waist that he would push her away, she did it anyway, feeling him stiffen in her arms.

But he didn't push her away. He didn't shift an inch. She tightened her arms around him and pressed her cheek against his chest. She could feel his heart beating. Thudding.

'May seventeenth is my birthday.'

A simple statement, but one Maisy felt soul-deep. *This* was what he did for his birthday. *This* was how he celebrated. Nobody even knew.

'I wish you'd told me,' was finally all she could think to say.

'It's just another day, Maisy.'

'But it brings back the past for you.'

It was the wrong thing to say. He took her by the elbows, physically setting her back from him.

'Listen, I know you mean well, *dushka*, but I don't need this.'

'This? Confiding in me?'

'Sympathy.' He gave her a crooked smile. 'I'm a big boy, Maisy.'

Yes, the little boy she wanted to comfort was all grown up. This was the result.

'Your sympathy is misplaced,' he said with finality. Then he turned away. 'I'll have some clothes sent down to you.'

'I'm not offering you sympathy,' she asserted shakily. 'Don't go like this, Alexei. Why won't you let me in?'

But part of her already knew why. She had never *really* been part of his inner circle to begin with.

'Maisy—' His big shoulders dropped and he swung around, a familiar rueful smile tugging at his mouth as if he was finding it difficult to be assertive with her.

It was then she recognised something that had been staring her in the face for a long time now if only she'd had the eyes to see it. She was the only person he did this for. Waited, listened, smiled. With everyone else it was clipped or cool or *über*sophisticated. The facade. With her he was like this… gentler, more human. She conjured up the Alexei she had first come up against in Lantern Square, hard as nails, taking no prisoners. Certainly not listening to her.

Well, he listened to her now. He'd been listening to her for weeks. She just hadn't been asking the right questions.

'Sometimes I feel I know next to nothing about you,' she admitted. 'Those men, Valery and Stiva, they're your family, aren't they? You must love them very much. And Leo—you must miss him.' She swallowed hard, took a deep breath and plunged in. 'But I'm here.' She paused to let that sink into his thick skull, then tunnelled on. 'I met Tara Mills this afternoon. I had this silly idea all your ex-girlfriends were perfect goddesses, but Tara was just…cold and angry. Boy, is she angry with you.'

'I didn't invite her, Maisy. She came with Dimitri Kouris.'

Alexei inserted this so fast Maisy almost smiled, and then reassured him she wasn't going to break into a jealous tirade.

In the end she shrugged. 'It doesn't matter either way.' And saying it made it so. 'But it made me think you couldn't have been happy with her, and you've seemed happy with me until today.'

'I am happy, Maisy.' He sounded so sincere, but he didn't make a move to touch her and his actions spoke louder than words.

She put her head to one side, studying him. 'You look about as happy as I feel, and that's saying something. You're an amazing man, Alexei Ranaevsky. I don't think I've stopped long enough to smell the coffee on that one. To have come to where you are, when someone like me wouldn't have had the resilience to even survive, it makes you pretty special.'

'So now I'm your hero?'

He gave her that cynical smile she'd seen him use on other people. But it didn't work on her. She *knew* him—or was coming to understand him. She loved him, and he was running scared from it. His past was so bleak he couldn't even recognise what was staring him in the face, but he sensed it, and it had him on the run.

'No, you're my boyfriend.'

That wiped the smile off his face. And there it was. The stretch between what she needed from him and what he was willing to offer.

She attempted to deflect his predictable reaction. 'Don't look so worried, Alexei. I know today's hard for you and I haven't made it any easier. But you could have confided in me just a little. I mean, who would I tell? Kostya?'

He cleared his throat. 'I didn't mean to isolate you.'

'You haven't. It's been nice, just the three of us, but I understand it's not enough for you, and I like your friends—or what I've seen of them. Ivanka has been very kind to me.'

'What's not enough for me?' Alexei zeroed in on the one thing she'd hoped would get lost in her rush of words.

'The three of us.' She swallowed. 'Me.' She hurried on. 'I didn't realise until today how different your life must have been before us. Leo and Anais lived very quietly at home. I didn't see this side of things. I mean, there were famous people on this boat, Alexei.'

Alexei's expression softened, some of the tension leaving him. 'They're just people, Maisy, and not particularly interesting for all their fame or money.'

'"A crowd" you called them. Why do you invite them?'

'Honestly, Maisy, after today I've got no idea. What a disaster.'

'I'm sorry I wrecked everything. You didn't need to empty the boat.'

'You didn't wreck anything,' he asserted in a driven undertone. 'I was a damned fool, dragging you along to this. I had an insane notion I could keep everything as it was, but that's impossible. You don't fit into this life, Maisy. You never did. And

I'm sorry you had such a lousy day. I take full responsibility for it.'

Maisy stared at him, trying to make sense of what he was saying above the roaring in her head. What did he mean she didn't fit into his life? Okay, she needed to get over this. She needed to put him first right now. Ignore the panic scrambling for a grip in her head and just focus. She'd been doing a good job of it. Dropping the ball now would be disastrous.

'I made an idiot of myself without any help from you, Alexei.'

'Nobody thinks you're an idiot, Maisy.' He closed the space between them and did what she had been wanting him to do all day. He framed her face, bent and kissed her. Gently, sweetly, far too briefly. 'I'll make it up to you tomorrow.'

Tomorrow. The future they didn't have.

She caught at his hand as he moved to step away. 'Where are you going?'

'You need clothes, *dushka*, and we need to get going. I've got guests, remember?'

Maisy flushed. Not *we've* got guests, just him. His guests. And she was holding him up.

'Maisy?' He captured her face between his big hands. 'This isn't about you. It's my problem. Okay?'

'No, Alexei, it's about *us*.' She pulled away from him. 'But I can say it till I'm blue in the face. You don't want it to be us. You're happier on your own. Go on, let me get dressed. We've got a long evening ahead and I'm not very happy with you right now.'

Alexei had the grace to lower his head. He looked about wiped out, Maisy realised, but he was right. He was a big boy. She had wounds to lick. He could look after himself.

CHAPTER ELEVEN

WHILST Maisy dressed Alexei returned to the boardroom to make a call in privacy to Valery at the house. He hadn't been in here since that dreary day when they had all gathered aboard *Firebird* to discuss Kostya. It felt like a lifetime ago.

Bursting into Lantern Square had changed his life irrevocably and there was no going back. He wouldn't want to go back. Maisy had changed everything.

You're my boyfriend. Those three words had summed up her simple, uncomplicated assessment of their relationship.

And, God help him, he'd been behaving like a boyfriend from day one in that park in Ravello, when she had snapped and crackled at him and, like the sucker he had never been, he'd followed her—tame as an alley cat offered food and a lap for the first time.

He'd convinced himself it would be casual sex to scratch the itch, but from the moment he'd seen her in his shirt, clear-eyed and standing up to him, casual had gone out of the window.

She'd known. Instinctively she'd known he wasn't the kind of man who would stick around. Every time they'd made love it had been behind her eyes. The question.

And finally all of it had come home to roost—what he had taught her to believe with his string of well-publicised affairs and his defensive habits. He'd thought he was protecting her, but all he'd been doing was protecting himself.

You don't want it to be us.

But, God help him, he did—and that was the black irony of

it all. He wanted a lifetime with Maisy. He'd just been on his own so long he didn't know how to go about it.

It was good to take her dampened dress off, her flimsy sandals, and just lie in a tub of clear warm water, her hair loose and submerged, her eyes closed. Downstairs there were guests to entertain, but Ivanka had assured her they were family and she was to have her bath, not worry about anything, and come down when she was ready.

Maria brought Kostya to her whilst she was dressing, and he helped her pick out a dress. She chose the cocktail dress she had brought from London.

The dress fell to her ankles, but was so sheer that no matter how she stood or moved it clung to her figure like a second skin. She waited to feel self-conscious but the feeling didn't come. Alexei had taught her the curvy body she had hidden under layers was sexy—no longer a source of unease but something to be celebrated.

There was a knock on her door. 'Come in.' She had expected Maria, looking for Kostya, but it was Stefania. She had swept her shoulder-length blond hair up and was wearing a glamorous seventies-style caftan, dripping in gold jewellery. Maisy loved the way these Russian women went completely over the top. It must be liberating.

'Wow, you are *so* not wearing that around my husband.'

Maisy turned in surprise, but Stefania was laughing.

'Oh, the baby!' She'd spotted Kostya.

Maisy introduced them, and Kostya allowed himself to be scooped up and admired.

'He's so beautiful, and you're a natural, Maisy. I don't know how I'm going to manage when I have one. I know everyone has a nanny, but I think Ivanka's on the right track. She does it all herself.'

'She's crazy,' said Maisy honestly. 'Everyone needs help.'

'But you brought up Kostya yourself. Alexei was just telling the boys you did it on your own for two years.'

Alexei?

Maisy was digesting this information when Stefania said critically, 'You need something around your neck. Show me your bling and we'll pick something out.'

'I don't have any bling,' Maisy confessed, trying to keep her voice light.

'You're kidding me? Alexei hasn't thrown open the gates of all the best jewellery stores? Maise, I'm gonna talk to that man.'

'No!' Maisy groaned. 'Please, Stefania, I honestly don't want jewellery.'

Stefania looked at her as if she had said *I don't need to breathe air.* 'Okay,' she said slowly, 'but you have to wear something, Maisy. Let me lend you one of my strings. I promise nothing over the top—something simple, ladylike. You do ladylike. I can tell.'

Within minutes Maisy was wearing a strand of pearls so pure they were iridescent. It would be hard to give them back.

Stefania smiled like a cat that had the cream at their reflections—herself so fair and slender, Maisy voluptuous, her long red-gold hair caught up in a single clasp. 'We look good. The guys will go off.'

It was seven o'clock when they went down, and past Kostya's bedtime, but Maisy knew instinctively part of the reason the Abramovs and Lievens were here was to see Leo's little boy. Maisy led him into the drawing room by the hand. She had dressed him up in his best royal-blue pyjamas suit, and with his angelic blond curls he looked delicious.

The glass of whisky in Alexei's hand slid from his grasp. He just caught it in time as Maisy strolled into the room holding one of Kostya's hands, Stefania the other. Maisy was elegance personified. She was wearing something white and it moved like water on her body, showcasing every curve. She'd pulled her titian hair up, which only made him want to take it down, and it drew attention to the delicate bone structure of her face. The artless, sunny girl he had first known might be lurking under the glamour of her evening dress, but it was a knowing woman whose eyes clashed with his across the room, then looked away to concentrate on his guests.

Her movements were unhurried as she smiled at everyone, answered questions about Kostya's development and hovered over him. Every shrug of her bare shoulders, every extension of a slender arm, turn of her head was seductive, drawing him across that room to the perimeter of where she held court, kneeling on the Aubusson rug, impossibly elegant even with a two-year-old squirming around her.

Valery and Stiva were riveted—and it wasn't to what Maisy was saying. When had she become this sophisticated woman? Had he not been paying attention? Or was it that it suited him to see her as sweet little Maisy, the girl he had collected from Lantern Square? Nothing ever stood still, and her words came back to smack him up the side of the head: *To have come to where you are, when someone like me wouldn't have had the resilience to even survive.*

Maisy underestimated herself. She had something he'd been lacking all his life: the courage to give of herself to others. He watched her—not only with Kostya, the child who wasn't her own yet whom she had taken into her heart, but with his friends, cheerful and generous despite her appalling day.

He'd been an absolute idiot.

Maisy kept an eye on Alexei as the evening wore on, but she didn't go out of her way to approach him. He needed to come to her, but as time wound away she was starting to feel as if that would never happen.

It was a revelation seeing him with people he cared about. This was how he had been with her and Kostya in these last weeks—generous and warm and loving. He got Sasha and Nicky, Ivanka's boys, set up with a games console in the entertainment room, and he scooped Kostya up to fly him through the air and fed him grapes, all the while carrying on a discussion with Valery about some American baseball team and a foolproof betting system.

He had a whole life she was only getting a glimpse of.

Well, he might not think she fitted into this life, but she had no intention of letting him go that easily.

After dinner, Maisy excused herself as coffee was served and sought the seclusion of the terrace. She could only hope Alexei would have the sense to follow her out—although given his unpredictable behaviour over the past couple of days she couldn't be sure.

Leaning against the railing, she took in deep sustaining breaths, trying to concentrate on the enviable view of blue sea. *Lap it up, Maisy*, a little voice taunted. *It's not going to last. Your days are numbered.*

Not without a fight, she responded, fisting her hands on top of the stone.

'Maisy.' His deep voice washed over her and she almost slumped with relief. She shut her eyes, wanting the peace to last, wanting him to be part of that peace but knowing he couldn't be.

He was too scared to love her.

'Go inside, Alexei. You've got guests.'

'Why are you out here on your own?'

'I just wanted some time out, okay?' She opened her eyes and made herself look at him. He was at least a metre away, arms folded, typical I-am-an-island stance. It was the same stance he had taken so many weeks ago, on that strange night when he had burst into her life. It was as if the past weeks had never happened. As if they had never even been lovers.

'Fine.' He didn't shift.

The cold sea wind had picked up and Maisy shivered. She could feel Alexei looking at her body, not very modestly wrapped in white silk and nothing else. She knew her nipples were prominent. She felt self-conscious about it now that his desire for her had so obviously cooled. Goose flesh had risen on her arms and she rubbed them.

Alexei shrugged off his jacket with a single movement and drew it around her shoulders, but otherwise he didn't touch her.

Maisy released a shuddery sigh, wondering why his gesture should touch her so deeply.

'You should be wearing more clothing,' was all he said, his head bent, his eyes intent upon hers.

Suddenly the wind was gone, the view blotted out. There was only Alexei, blocking out the world, and Maisy was thrown back to Lantern Square when she had stepped into his arms and he had picked her up and branded her. There was no other way to describe it, and she was still wearing that brand. She was his. From then on she'd always been his.

'Please talk to me, Alexei.'

'It's not the time or place, Maisy.'

Her temper snapped. 'Too bad—because I've got a few things to say. First of all, I love you. I'm in love with you. And I'm stupid with it—because, honestly, any other woman would have seen the writing on the wall long before I did.'

He was silent. Maisy almost swore.

'You don't have anything to say to me?'

'This "stupid" love…' his voice was low, almost fractured '…did it make its appearance after Ivanka told you my sob story or before? Don't tell me you fell for me when I burst into the kitchen at Lantern Square and terrified the life out of you?'

How on earth had they arrived back at that? Maisy shook her head. It was either that or shake him.

'Right now I have no idea why I love you,' she slung at him heatedly. 'Maybe it's the multiple orgasms.'

His savage laugh ripped through the tension holding Maisy in place.

'I know you *think* you love me, Maisy,' he said, with a smile that didn't reach his eyes. 'I'm basically the first man you've been intimate with. It's understandable you imagine you feel this way.'

Think. *Imagine.* She wanted to claw his eyes out.

'Basically?' she said, stony cold.

Something flashed through Alexei's expression, leaving his eyes almost feral. 'He didn't give you an orgasm.'

Maisy rotated her fists. 'How do you know?'

He moved so fast she didn't even have a chance to resist. His hands were around her arms, pinning her, his mouth hot and hard, demanding a submission she wasn't going to give him. But the shock of it, the longing to be in his arms and provoke a response from him, undid her. She gave a soft little moan and kissed him back.

He drew back, satisfied, releasing her. 'That's how I know, *dushka*. Only me.'

'And when did you realise that, Alexei?' she flashed back at him, wiping her mouth and gaining satisfaction from the narrowing of his eyes. *Yes, Alexei, look—I'm wiping your low-down kiss off me.* 'Today? Yesterday? Last week?'

'Seven weeks ago,' he growled. 'You've been in my bed six weeks, five days.'

He surprised her with the knowledge he had kept count. A tiny flicker of hope formed in its wake.

'It took me a full seven days to make my move,' he continued. 'Slow, considering I could have had you that first night in London.'

The light went out. Maisy struggled to keep her nerve, but he had never been like this with her before. He could be cold, but he had never been crass.

'What do you mean?' She hated the note of desperation that had crept into her voice.

He heard it. She saw the bleak satisfaction enter his hard eyes. 'You heard me. I seem to remember you kissing me back, Maisy, your legs around my waist. You were there all the way.'

'No, that's not true. You're twisting it. I was so ashamed. I couldn't believe I'd let you do that—' She broke off, seeing triumph flash painfully across his face.

Idiot. She had blundered and said what he had been pushing her to admit. She'd allowed her own vulnerability to him to distract her from what was at issue. Maisy suddenly realised what this was all about and she shut her mouth.

'*Da*, you were so ashamed you couldn't wait to dive into bed with me the day I turned up here. It must have been hard, *dushka*, all that waiting. Explains why you were so easy to warm up the minute your back hit that mattress.'

Maisy made herself stay expressionless and stone-still, all the while silently repeating, *He doesn't mean it. He doesn't mean it.*

He was waiting for her to respond. Waiting for her to do something. But Maisy held her ground. And the longer she stood there, staring stonily back at him, the more pronounced the ticking of the nerve below his jaw became. He was *so* stubborn, she thought, and *hard*. *Harder than me*, thought Maisy desperately, and he could so very well win because of it.

Cursing in Russian, he cut the air with a frustrated gesture of his hand, reeling around and walking away from her. Then he spun and said harshly, 'This is who I am, Maisy. I'm the one who turned your life upside down, who railroaded you into a sexual relationship—who drags you all over the continent and dresses you up like a doll, parades you on a boat as if you're a goddamned trophy.'

Maisy could only stare at him and listen and ignore what he was saying.

He was shouting at her now. 'I'm a class-A bastard, Maisy. That's my reputation. You seem to be the only person on the planet who isn't aware of that.'

She had never seen him like this. He had been angry before, but always in control, always measuring his response. That control had splintered, but the anger wasn't directed at her. She knew him now. It was directed at himself.

But she had some of her own to serve up.

'Listen to me, you stupid man. For your information, I would *never* have let things go that far that night in London.' Her voice rose strong above the hum of the wind and the ocean. 'The only reason I ever slept with you here was because *I* wanted to, and it was everything I dreamed of—because you were sweet and kind and considerate, everything you claim you're not. But I'm tired of being on the outside of your life, and I will never, *never* forgive you for throwing my feelings back in my face unless you get down on your sorry knees and beg my forgiveness, and then work your behind off making it up to me.'

Face flushed, body trembling Maisy took a backward step. 'Starting right now.'

Then she swung away and headed inside. She'd had her say. At last. Whatever happened next was up to him.

It occurred to her that his friends had probably heard a great deal of what had been said—especially the last part where she'd been shouting—but suddenly she didn't care. She felt almost light-headed with emotion. If strangers thought she was a fool, what did it matter? She was fighting for the life and the man she wanted, and she refused to be ashamed of that.

She accepted a glass of iced tea from Valery as she sat down, who murmured, close to her ear, 'We're rooting for you, Maisy, and by the way I love the dress.'

Maisy went red to the roots of her hair, but the adrenaline enabled her to smile and shrug.

'Valery, stop flirting with Maisy,' said Ivanka mildly.

Alexei had come into the room looking like thunder, hands hooked into his pockets. He stood at the end of the sofa, staring at her.

Maisy shrugged off his jacket and threw it at him.

Stiva clapped his hands and dropped into the chair opposite Maisy. 'Now, *this* I've gotta see.'

'You're toast,' said Valery, handing Alexei a glass of brandy.

Alexei ignored it. 'Maisy, upstairs—now.'

'No.' She crossed her legs and concentrated on her drink. She could literally *feel* Alexei breathing. 'But if you're the—what was it?—*class-A bastard* you claim to be why don't you just drag me out of here by my hair?' She blinked innocently up at him, her fingernails scoring her palms.

She heard Stefania's sharp intake of breath, and then the

solid warmth of Ivanka's leg and hip as she slid onto the sofa close up beside her. She remembered her assurance— 'I've got your back'—on *Firebird*, and wanted to tell her it was fine. Alexei wasn't about to do anything so primitive. Except she really didn't know.

And the not knowing sped up her heart.

Alexei towered over her, laser-blue eyes fixed on her alone.

'You really want to have this out here and now?'

There was a warning in his eyes even as his voice remained cool, direct. Public voice, private eyes.

She flashed back to that morning when he had towered over her as she'd sat on the terrace, Kostya in her arms. Literally crushing her heart with his careless assertion about other women.

Except it hadn't been careless. He had used it as a weapon to keep her at a distance and more importantly, it hadn't been true.

Was he lying to her now? Was he doing it to push her away?

'Alexei thinks I'm too good for him,' she said out loud.

'Yeah, because you are,' said Stiva jovially.

'Stiva!' Ivanka glowered at him.

'He tried to make me his mistress, but I'm not. I'm his girlfriend. Not that he's ever even brought me a bunch of flowers.'

'Or bling,' put in Stefania.

'I don't mind about the jewellery. I told him I didn't want any. I didn't say anything about flowers, though.'

Maisy was talking to her glass. She knew in revealing what was between them before others she was taking a chance with this most private and closely guarded of men. These people were his family, but that probably made it worse. Yet what choice was he giving her? And what had she to lose? She needed to push him. For him to see he was surrounded by people who loved him. *She* loved him. She wanted him to love *her*.

'A single rose from the garden would have done, or maybe some wildflowers from the roadside—' She broke off as her glass was snatched from her and then big familiar hands closed around her waist.

He plucked her from the sofa and she wound her arms around his neck and let him carry her, as docile as she had been that morning when he had come to seduce her.

'Like I said,' Valery commented dryly, 'toast.'

Maisy threw an anxious look at Alexei's face so close to her own. He wasn't angry. He was determined, but it wasn't anger he was radiating—it was something else. Something that made her instinctively cling to him.

'Where are we going?' she demanded, although it was clear he was taking her upstairs.

'Why can't we have fights like that?' Stefania's high voice floated after them.

Maisy suspected she was about to be ravished on that big bed upstairs and little else. A miracle would have to take place to get Alexei to talk, and she was just about out of pulling miracles from her sleeve.

Maria appeared at the top of the stairs and Maisy struggled to be put down, but Alexei held fast.

'I have bad news for you, Alexei,' she said simply. 'The *bambino* wants his *mamma*.'

Alexei paused on the threshold of the nursery, expecting a difficult struggle to calm Kostya down. It was going to take many months to convince a child of this age his parents weren't coming back. He'd been through it all with the psychologist.

The boy was with the night nanny, his little face red and screwed up with crying. It had been a long, awful day, but it was the first time Alexei had felt truly hopeless. He couldn't communicate with Maisy, and he couldn't protect Kostya from this.

'Mama!' He sniffled, big eyes latching onto Maisy and not letting go.

She moved swiftly to him, took the child into her arms and

settled into a chair. His cries subsided almost instantly as he buried his hot face in her neck and clung.

Alexei swore softly under his breath. He'd been blind. It wasn't Anais the boy wanted. It was Maisy. She had taken the role of Kostya's mother from the beginning.

It had always been Maisy.

It was peaceful in the nursery, but Maisy knew what awaited her outside. She'd forced this confrontation and now she was going to get it. Ready or not.

Alexei was watching them, arms folded over his chest, leaning against the bureau. He hadn't turned tail and run in the face of the infant's tears. For a man with no experience of children he'd adapted quickly and irrevocably to the fact he had one in his life. It was clearly just *women* he had a commitment problem with.

Kostya's body was sleep-heavy, and Maisy knew the moment had arrived. She moved reluctantly to stand.

'Here, let me take him.'

Alexei's deep voice had the volume turned down, but its impact shuddered through Maisy as she gave up the baby to him. He lifted Kostya from her arms with a practised move that caught at Maisy's raw emotions. His eyes flickered to hers. They had done this so many times, she realized. Like a tag team—*like parents*. She saw acknowledgement of this in his expression for the first time.

Shaken, Maisy fetched Kostya's favourite blanket, draping it over his sleeping body, and then without saying a word or sparing a glance for Alexei she slipped outside.

She was halfway down the hall when she heard the nursery door click shut, and then Alexei's hushed voice whipped her around. 'Not so fast.'

In that instant Maisy realised she was actually running away from him. She was behaving like a scared little mouse—the timid girl who had started at St Bernice's all those years ago and looked to Anais to fight her battles. She was a grown woman now, and if anything the past few weeks had taught her she could handle one large, moody Russian male—except this time she needed to do it without sex muddying the waters and confusing the issues.

He stalked towards her, the down lights on the walls throwing his shadow so that he seemed to increase in height as he stood over her.

Maisy's trembling hands automatically found her hips. 'If you think I'm going to jump into bed with you and have mad, passionate, angry sex so you can put this behind us and just go on as before—'

'We've done that, Maisy, and moved on from it,' he interrupted.

The fact that he was on the same page with her brought Maisy up short.

'What I want to know is what was that about downstairs?'

Testosterone was pounding out of him, and Maisy was so distracted by the urge to press herself up against him she had trouble concentrating.

'The stuff about the jewellery,' he clarified, his accent clotting up the words.

Maisy shook herself. She was doing the very thing she had warned him against.

'I'm sorry for embarrassing you,' she answered. 'But I was very angry—'

'You didn't embarrass me, Maisy,' he broke in impatiently. 'I want to know what it was about.' He seemed to close in around her. 'What do you want from me? I'll bring in a jeweller tomorrow—you can have whatever you want.'

'I don't *want* jewellery!' she exploded. 'Oh, how can you be so ridiculously obtuse?'

'*I'm* obtuse? You made it very clear in Paris that anything—*anything*—I bought for you was payment. Can you blame me for being wary about putting anything around your neck?'

'So it's all *my* fault? I don't know what I'm doing, Alexei. Have you ever thought about that? It's not like I've ever been a rich man's mistress before. Forgive me if I make mistakes. You never gave me a rule book.'

'You're not my mistress,' he said firmly. 'I have never, *never* treated you as a mistress.'

'You dress me; you chauffeur me around in limos; you keep me separate from your working life. Until now I've never met any of your friends. What else am I?'

'I'm looking after you. You and Kostya. The three of us.'

'No, Alexei,' she said softly, sadly. 'It's just you.'

Her words fell like stones into the silence. Maisy's emotions trembled with the weight of the impact of what she had said. He looked so lost, her big, steely take-no-prisoners Alexei. *He needs me so badly*, Maisy realized, and it gave her the courage to go on.

'That's what you do, Alexei, to protect yourself. You shut yourself off. You choose women who pick you because of what you can give them—*stuff*, luxury and publicity—and that way it's never about emotions. And God forbid anyone asks for more than that—falls in love with you because you're so scared to be vulnerable to someone, to trust and lay yourself open to being abandoned and hurt again.'

Alexei said something harsh in Russian. The sound of it was enough to dry up the words in Maisy's mouth. He was very pale and very menacing in the down lights, his shadow pressing down on her.

'I *know* I would never abandon a child who needed me,' she pressed. 'Anais never bonded with Kostya. It was all I could do to get her to be there in the morning when I got him up. I *do* know what it is to be abandoned because I watched it happen to a child I love. It made it impossible for me not to do everything I could to care for Kostya. And you clearly felt the same way—because you came and rescued him, because that's how you show love. You offer protection. But I don't need your protection. I'm not two years old. I need you to open yourself up to me and trust me not to take advantage of you, not to hurt you.'

'What is it you want from me?' he said in a low voice. 'Name it and I'll do it.'

He still wasn't prepared to risk himself. Maisy felt the weight of the only choice left to her bearing down. She had to leave him and go back to London. She had done all she could to make Alexei see what was standing in front of him. She loved him, but she didn't know if he was ever going to change. Nothing she had said seemed to have made a whit of difference.

She needed to protect herself emotionally or he would destroy her. It was the only way forward for both of them. It meant she could very possibly lose him, but what choice had he left her?

She had to risk herself, because he wouldn't. 'Anything?' she whispered.

He turned, his features entirely Tartar, menacing, miserable. It broke her heart.

'Let me take Kostya back to Lantern Square.' Her voice dropped an octave as she felt the world shift and tumble away from her feet. 'Let me go.'

He flinched as if she had struck him. 'Kostya is my responsibility, not yours,' he said, in a strained voice she barely recognised.

'I can't leave him,' she whispered.

He turned away from her. She could see all the muscles in his shoulders converge on that one point at the nape of his neck where she used to link her hands. Those shoulders rose and fell.

'You're the only mother he's ever known,' Alexei said in a low voice, as if speaking to himself. 'It took me until tonight to recognise that.'

Maisy felt time stop as he turned slowly, his blue eyes so dark in the down light they seemed black. His eyes held hers, as if in challenge. 'All things considered, I think going back to Lantern Square might be exactly what you need, *dushka*.

But I am in Kostya's life. You're never going to be free of me whilst you're with him.'

'I'm packing now,' she answered, swallowing hard. 'And I'm going first thing in the morning. Can you organise that for Kostya and me?'

'*Da*. But this isn't over, Maisy.'

She shrugged, her throat clenching with the effort to keep her emotions in check. There was nothing more to say. She'd said it all. It was up to him now.

CHAPTER TWELVE

MAISY heard the bells chime over the door. No clients had been scheduled today, so she expected it was Alice, back early from the school run.

She put down her pen and got up to put the kettle on, pouring Earl Grey tea leaves into the pot. Her eyes were a little sore from peering at the laptop screen, but Alice would be pleased when she heard her good news. She'd managed to source French *valenciennes* lace and get it under price.

Alice's little shop was a dream come true for Maisy. After landing back in Lantern Square, her first week had been absorbed by resettling Kostya back into a routine and organising a crèche for him before she got stuck into looking for a job.

It had been whilst she was filling in forms with a couple of the other mothers at the crèche around the corner that she had got talking to Alice. With her youngest now at school she had taken her millinery business off the internet and into a store, and hadn't been looking forward to toiling through the pile of applications she'd received for an assistant's job. Maisy had seen her chance and taken it.

All the role required was sourcing materials, a little bookkeeping work and chasing up orders three times a week. It was perfect.

It also kept her busy. Today was a record day for her. It was the first morning she'd woken up and her first thought hadn't been of Alexei. No doubt she'd think about him some time today—slide into a little reverie, maybe even soak her pillow tonight in tears—but it had only been a month, and she didn't expect to get over him any time soon.

What mattered was that during the day she was her own woman. She had already established a small circle of friends through Kostya's activities and her own work here in the shop. She went out to the cinema, she shopped, she met other people for coffee. It was simple and restrained, but it suited her. That lifestyle of limos and hotels and personal shoppers had never sat well with her. This was on her own terms, and if it didn't include Alexei it wasn't through any lack of trying. She'd told him what she wanted from him. It was becoming eminently clear he couldn't give it to her.

She turned to make room at the table for Alice, and almost tripped. Standing in the doorway was not slender, elfin-faced Alice but six and a half feet of Russian male—the same male she had been alternately longing for and cursing over for four long weeks. He was wearing simple and expensively tailored dark trousers and a white shirt open at the throat, and he looked every inch of what he was: a ruthless, sophisticated guy. So out of place amongst the lace and frou-frou of a ladies' hat shop it was almost humorous.

Almost.

Alexei noted the wide eyes, the pink cheeks, the shock, and took immediate advantage.

No sense in wasting time.

He had known Maisy had garnered herself a job virtually the minute she'd walked back in the door of Lantern Square. He knew she was rarely home, that she took Kostya with her here to the shop when he wasn't in the crèche, or on play dates to various addresses over London. She preferred the bus to expensive cabs, and she went to the cinema most Thursday nights.

The millinery shop was within walking distance of the house and Alexei had come on foot, turning over the bare facts of Maisy's existence since she'd vanished from his sight.

It all sounded completely ordinary, and he knew Maisy must love it.

But *this* he hadn't expected. The small, elegant shopfront, the tinkle of bells as he entered, the subtle fragrance in the air that reminded him of daisies and blue skies. He was rendered overgrown and slightly clumsy in this rarefied atmosphere, and he wondered with a smile if *any* man had dared step inside.

According to his report Maisy worked here on Thursday afternoons until four. He could hear somebody moving around at the rear of the shop and he strode across the shiny black and white parquet, sidling around the counter, noting the lack of security cameras or any security devices at all. He frowned.

She was standing with her back to him, head slightly bent. From the top of her bright head down to the elegant pale blue sheath dress, cinched at her small waist and clutching her rounded hips, down the seams of her pale stockings to the pretty French heel of her shoes, she was all lovely lines and femininity.

Then she turned, and those cinnamon eyes flared, and her face happened to him all over again.

But she didn't do any of the things he might have expected her to. A gasp, a frown, or more preferably throwing herself into his arms. She simply stood there, slender arms at her sides, bright titian ringlets framing a solemn expression tinged with a little wonder. She didn't make a move towards him, but nor did she move away.

It shouldn't have come as a surprise. She'd been magnificent in those last couple of days they'd had together, lifting the bar on their relationship so high he'd been unable to cross it. Exerting her own will, matching it against his. Few men had the guts for it, but she hadn't blinked. Then again, those men didn't burrow up against him in bed and lift soft eyes that turned all his intentions her way.

Yet, unlike every other woman he'd come across, she hadn't used sex to manipulate him. She'd given him an ultimatum, and she'd stuck by it. He hadn't known she'd had it in her. All he'd seen was the sweet, artless girl he had fallen in love with on sight. But, damn, he respected her for it. And she'd been right.

'Alexei.'

'Hello, Maisy.'

Looking up into the familiar, beautiful lines of his face, she struggled to find the man whose wretched eyes had haunted her dreams for weeks now. He had returned to being the hard-edged, sophisticated guy who had come bursting into her kitchen and changed her life for ever. Except when his eyes rested on her a little smile she recognised tugged on the corner of his lips, and his blue eyes softened on hers with a question.

Alexei Ranaevsky didn't ask questions. He issued directives.

Everybody knew that. But Maisy knew differently.

It hadn't been that way between them from the moment he'd seized hold of her arm in that park in Ravello. She remembered how his body had actually been vibrating, and in her ignorance she had thought him angry. It hadn't been anger, and it had been more than desire for her. He had felt the connection and it had thrown him as much as it had thrown her, and they'd both been tumbling down the long hill of it ever since.

Maisy knew where she wanted to land, but it had been almost a whole month and he hadn't called her—he hadn't let her know how he was doing.

Every night he spoke to Kostya on the phone. It was a regular six o'clock routine. She would pick up, would hear his voice, deep and caressing, saying, 'Maisy,' and she would reply, 'Kostya's right here,' not trusting herself to even say his name. She would sit beside the little boy as he chattered exuberantly, the faint sound of Alexei's voice all she'd allow herself. There was always the temptation as Kostya said his goodbyes not to press 'end' and to speak to him herself—but what would she say? *I love you. I want to come back to you.* But it wasn't her call. Alexei was a smart guy. If he had something to say to her he would have rung her and said it.

Actually, knowing the man as she did, he would have hopped on a plane and said it to her face.

And here he was.

In those last days together she had taken command not only of herself but of whatever was between them. Having him suddenly here, filling up the tiny space with his presence, it felt as if Alexei had seized it back, and Maisy felt slightly on the back foot.

'What are you doing here?' She sounded breathless to her own ears.

'I've been to Lantern Square to check the security.'

It wasn't what she'd expected him to say, and something small and bright that had lit in her mind at the sight of him went out.

'I had it changed whilst you were with me in Ravello.'

He made it sound as if those two months had been merely a holiday. Next he would make some comment about her tan fading—that was if she'd even had a tan. Maisy stopped gazing up adoringly and pulled herself together.

'I really don't think it's necessary,' she said, as coolly as she could manage. 'I don't think Kostya's in any danger.' But even as she spoke she could have kicked herself. She knew exactly why he was so security conscious. Every time he looked at Kostya he saw himself and what he had never had.

'Not just Kostya. I want you to be safe, Maisy.'

'Me? Why would anyone want to hurt me?'

'I don't think anyone wants to hurt you. I just—' He broke off, running a hand through his hair as he smiled at her ruefully. 'I'm doing that thing you say I do. I'm showing you how much I love you by protecting you.'

Maisy was glad she had a table behind her to steady herself against.

'I'm on my knees, Maisy.' His voice was a whole octave deeper. 'I'm begging you to forgive me. I want to take you and Kostya home with me to Ravello, where you both belong. I want us to be a family.'

Maisy's mouth had run dry and she moistened her lips. 'It took you almost four weeks to decide this?'

He was suddenly filling the tiny private space, and Maisy had nowhere else to go.

'Has it been so hard without me?'

'No,' she lied.

'I haven't been able to breathe,' he confessed roughly. 'It hurts every time I do.'

Me too, her heart whispered.

'Four weeks, Alexei.' It came out jerkily.

'And look what you've done with it.'

He smiled at her then, that slow smile she loved so well. She wanted to smile back, but she felt if she did her entire life would go land-sliding towards him and she didn't want that quite yet.

'You were too scared to love me,' she risked saying.

'Precious little scares me, *dushka*, but you had me on the back foot from the moment we met,' he confessed—so candidly she couldn't help edging towards him. 'That day on the yacht, Maisy, it all came apart. When we were travelling together it was easier to keep you tucked away, out of sight. I understand you felt marginalized, but that's not what I was thinking. You belonged to me—a better me—not the man who keeps all the financial balls spinning. I didn't want to let the air in on that rarefied atmosphere we had. It was so precious to me.'

Maisy had gone very still. She hadn't considered it from that angle before. It had never occurred to her that *she* was the good thing in his life. All she had imagined was her inability to fit in.

'I wish you'd told me,' she answered softly.

'Hell, I hardly framed it as an idea to myself. I was running on instinct, Maisy. But I knew it wasn't fair to you, so I decided to use *Firebird* as an introduction.'

'Except it meant then that in everyone else's eyes I was your mistress.' It still stung, and she wasn't going to hide that from him.

Alexei's blue eyes sought hers earnestly. 'The people who mattered didn't think that, Maisy. Anyone with eyes in their head could see how much I loved you.'

He'd said he loved her. Twice. Maisy couldn't help reaching up to lay her hand against his chest. The heat and solidity of him felt like utter security.

'I realised I was pushing you away when all I wanted was intimacy. I just didn't know how to protect myself and still have everything with you.'

Maisy touched him with her other hand, just resting it on his chest, her fingers slightly curling around the fabric. He seemed to feel so guilty, and she didn't want that.

'I knew I'd made a colossal mistake,' he said roughly. 'But that meant re-evaluating everything I knew and I was struggling with it. When Leo died I was lost.'

His heavy sigh had her hands tightening on his shirt.

'Nothing felt right,' he said simply. 'And then I found you and it all fell into place.'

His eyes hadn't left hers once. His sincerity was making it difficult for her not to respond, yet she wanted to hear all of this. Desperately.

'Watching you with Kostya, seeing how much of a mother you've clearly been to him from birth, and then having you open yourself up to me. We're both very lucky males to have you in our lives.'

Maisy bit her lip.

'It just took me a little time to adjust, and you kept pushing,' he confessed with a half-smile, then reached out and gently thumbed the line puckering between her brows. 'I'm glad you did, *dushka*. You made me face a few home truths. It was only when you made it clear what you wanted that I realised I'd been kidding myself.'

'I didn't think I had much to lose,' she confessed. 'You would have pushed me away anyway. You didn't want me to love you.'

He framed her face with his big hands. 'Maisy Edmonds, as fast as I was backing up, I had no intention of losing you.'

'You sent me back here.'

'You asked me to. I gave you what you wanted.'

'If you'd argued with me I would only have resented you,' she admitted honestly, more to herself than him. 'I needed to find myself again, Alexei. I needed to see if I could do it on my own.'

'Look at you.' He gave her that slow smile that made her thighs turn to water and everything tingle. 'The working girl.'

'Damn right.'

Alexei was tangling one hand through her curls. 'Now I've come for what I want.'

'You're very sure of yourself,' Maisy murmured, thrilled.

'*Da*, but you like me that way, *dushka*.'

'Bossy.'

'Taking you over, not giving you a choice.'

He leaned in and kissed her, and his tenderness was the undoing of her.

He drew back enough to say, 'But you've got all the choices now, Maisy. Come back with me, be a family with me; share your life with me. You can have it all, *dushka*.'

Maisy gripped hold of his shirt front, making a mess of the sleek tailored lines.

'I want to be with you, Alexei.'

It was an echo from another time, another place, and he recognised it immediately. By a fountain in a garden, when they'd both been reeling from the impact of what being together might mean.

He knew exactly what it meant. The rest of his life was standing in front of him.

Gently disengaging her hands, he dropped down onto one knee and looked up at her. 'I love you, Maisy Edmonds. Would you do me the honour of becoming my wife?'

Maisy stared at him for what felt like the longest time. He was in love with her and he wanted to marry her.

'Oh, yes, I'm sure I can do that,' she responded, a big smile breaking out across her face.

Maisy's eye caught the glitter of the ring he had produced and she swallowed hard.

'Take a deep breath,' he murmured. 'I know you're not that keen on diamonds.'

She had a hard time not snatching it from him. Then she realised the ring was glittering because Alexei's hands were shaking.

Alexei slid the ring onto her finger. It fitted almost perfectly.

'It's so beautiful,' she whispered. '*You're* so beautiful.'

'That's my line, *dushka*.'

He was on his feet, gathering her into his arms. The relief on his face was almost as touching as his sweet, old-fashioned proposal. Maria had once told her that underneath all the surface swagger Alexei was as traditional as they came, but she hadn't listened.

She was listening now.

'I love you, Maisy.' His eyes deep in hers, his voice was heartbreakingly sincere. 'Let's go home.'

* * * * *

CLASSIC

Harlequin
Presents

COMING NEXT MONTH from Harlequin Presents® EXTRA
AVAILABLE APRIL 10, 2012

#193 SAVAS'S WILDCAT
Return of the Rebels
Anne McAllister

#194 THE DEVIL AND MISS JONES
Return of the Rebels
Kate Walker

#195 THE EX WHO HIRED HER
The Ex Files
Kate Hardy

#196 THE EX FACTOR
The Ex Files
Anne Oliver

COMING NEXT MONTH from Harlequin Presents®
AVAILABLE APRIL 24, 2012

#3059 RETURN OF THE MORALIS WIFE
Jacqueline Baird

#3060 THE PRICE OF ROYAL DUTY
The Santina Crown
Penny Jordan

#3061 A DEAL AT THE ALTAR
Marriage by Command
Lynne Graham

#3062 A NIGHT OF LIVING DANGEROUSLY
Jennie Lucas

#3063 A WILD SURRENDER
Anne Mather

#3064 GIRL BEHIND THE SCANDALOUS REPUTATION
Scandal in the Spotlight
Michelle Conder

You can find more information on upcoming Harlequin®
titles, free excerpts and more at www.Harlequin.com.

HPCNM0412

REQUEST YOUR FREE BOOKS!

◆Harlequin *Presents*

PASSION GUARANTEED SEDUCTION

2 FREE NOVELS PLUS
2 FREE GIFTS!

YES! Please send me 2 FREE Harlequin Presents® novels and my 2 FREE gifts (gifts are worth about $10). After receiving them, if I don't wish to receive any more books, I can return the shipping statement marked "cancel." If I don't cancel, I will receive 6 brand-new novels every month and be billed just $4.30 per book in the U.S. or $4.99 per book in Canada. That's a saving of at least 14% off the cover price! It's quite a bargain! Shipping and handling is just 50¢ per book in the U.S. and 75¢ per book in Canada.* I understand that accepting the 2 free books and gifts places me under no obligation to buy anything. I can always return a shipment and cancel at any time. Even if I never buy another book, the two free books and gifts are mine to keep forever.

106/306 HDN FERQ

Name _____
(PLEASE PRINT)

Address _____ Apt. #

City _____ State/Prov. _____ Zip/Postal Code

Signature (if under 18, a parent or guardian must sign)

Mail to the **Reader Service:**
IN U.S.A.: P.O. Box 1867, Buffalo, NY 14240-1867
IN CANADA: P.O. Box 609, Fort Erie, Ontario L2A 5X3

Not valid for current subscribers to Harlequin Presents books.

**Are you a current subscriber to Harlequin Presents books
and want to receive the larger-print edition?
Call 1-800-873-8635 or visit www.ReaderService.com.**

* Terms and prices subject to change without notice. Prices do not include applicable taxes. Sales tax applicable in N.Y. Canadian residents will be charged applicable taxes. Offer not valid in Quebec. This offer is limited to one order per household. All orders subject to credit approval. Credit or debit balances in a customer's account(s) may be offset by any other outstanding balance owed by or to the customer. Please allow 4 to 6 weeks for delivery. Offer available while quantities last.

Your Privacy—The Reader Service is committed to protecting your privacy. Our Privacy Policy is available online at www.ReaderService.com or upon request from the Reader Service.

We make a portion of our mailing list available to reputable third parties that offer products we believe may interest you. If you prefer that we not exchange your name with third parties, or if you wish to clarify or modify your communication preferences, please visit us at www.ReaderService.com/consumerchoice or write to us at Reader Service Preference Service, P.O. Box 9062, Buffalo, NY 14269. Include your complete name and address.

HPI1B

Stop The Press! *Crown Prince in Shock Marriage*

When Crown Prince Alessandro of Santina
proposes to paparazzi favorite Allegra Jackson
it promises to be *the* social event of the decade!

Discover all 8 stories in the scandalous
new miniseries THE SANTINA CROWN
from Harlequin Presents®!

***

Enjoy this sneak peek from Penny Jordan's
THE PRICE OF ROYAL DUTY,
book 1 in THE SANTINA CROWN *miniseries.*

"DON'T YOU THINK you're being a tad dramatic?" he
asked her in a wry voice.

"I'm not being dramatic," she defended herself. "Surely
I should have some rights as a person, a human being, some
say in my own fate, instead of having my future decided
for me by my father. To endure marriage to a man who has
simply agreed to marry me because he wants an heir, and to
whom my father has virtually auctioned me off in exchange
for a royal alliance."

"I should have thought such a marriage would suit you,
Sophia. After all, it's well documented that your own chosen lifestyle involves something very similar, when it comes
to bed hopping."

A body blow indeed, and one that drove the blood from
Sophia's face and doubled the pain in her heart. It shouldn't
matter what Ash thought of her. That was not part of her
plan. But still his denunciation of her hurt, and it wasn't one

EXP0412

she could defend herself against. Not without telling him far more than she wanted him to know.

"Then you thought wrong" was all she could permit herself to say. "That is not the kind of marriage I want. I can't bear the thought of this marriage." Her panic and fear were there in her voice; even she could hear it herself, so how much more obvious must it be to Ash?

She must try to stay calm. Not even to Ash could she truly explain the distaste, the loathing, the fear she had of being forced by law to give herself in a marriage bed in the most intimate way possible when… No, that was one secret that she must keep no matter what, just as she had already kept it for so long. "Please, Ash, I'm begging you for your help."

Will Ash discover Sophia's secret?
Find out in THE PRICE OF ROYAL DUTY
by
USA TODAY *bestselling author*
Penny Jordan

Book 1 of THE SANTINA CROWN miniseries available May 2012 from Harlequin Presents®!